# The Spirit in the Stick

Published by Duffy Publishing.

The author wishes to acknowledge and thank the following publishers and individuals for permission to quote their work: The University of North Carolina Press (*In the Hands of Providence* by Alice Rains Trulock © 1992), The United States Naval Academy *Lucky Bag*, Bartleby.com, Inc. ("The Bivouac of the Dead"), Captain Gerry Coffee (*Beyond Survival* © 1990), Dover Publications, Inc. (*Myths of the Cherokee* by James Mooney © 1996), Dr. Thomas Vennum (*American Indian Lacrosse: Little Brother of War* © 1994 by the Smithsonian Institution), Fairview Press (*The Book of Positive Quotations*, compiled and arranged by John Cook. Copyright © 1993 Rubicon Press, Inc.), John Wiley & Sons, Inc. (*Lacrosse* by W. Kelso Morrill © 1966 by The Roland Press Company), Doubleday, a division of Random House, Inc. (*Anne Frank: The Diary of a Young Girl* by Anne Frank, translated by B.M. Mooyaart—Doubleday, © 1952 by Otto H. Frank), Scott Russell Sanders (*Hunting for Hope* © 1998).

Cover art and design by Mike Gottleib USNA '70, G3 Communications, Inc.
Copyright © 2004 by Neil Duffy
Manuscript Edition First Printing May 2003

ISBN: 0-9753686-0-5

# The Spirit in the Stick

Neil Duffy

Duffy Publishing
Virginia Beach, Virginia

*For*
*my late mother,*
*Teresa Cassidy Duffy*

**In Honor of**
*Dr. John H. Tucker, Jr.*

**And in Memory of**
*MIDN 2/C Bill Sisler, USNA '83*
*LT Robert Bianchi, USNA '83*
*DeShannon Artemis "D.A." Taylor*
*John Krumenacker*
*Ken Taylor*
*Dave Anderson*
*Richie Lovell*
*Dixon Rollins*
*CDR Kevin Bianchi, USNA '85*

# Introduction

"Lacrosse is one of the great team games on the American sports scene. Nearly everyone who has played it or watched it as a spectator loves the game. Lacrosse gets in your blood because it is such a fast-moving and exciting sport." My love of lacrosse remains as strong today as it was when I wrote those words almost 30 years ago. In the last three decades lacrosse's popularity has grown by leaps and bounds, and though today's players, whether male of female, are more skilled and better conditioned than ever before, the Game is still the Game.

The magic of lacrosse has captivated me—heart, mind, and soul for over 60 years. It is in *my* blood. The lessons the game has taught me have guided me all my life. The game has connected me with thousands of people who share a love for the game, resulting in lasting friendships with players, coaches, and their families.

Lacrosse, considered the oldest sport known to North America, is a game rich in tradition and history. Yet there is very little lacrosse literature. So it is with great pride that I introduce *The Spirit in the Stick*. This work is, to the best of my knowledge, the first and only of its kind. Its story is so deep and powerful that it is sure to *enrich* everyone who reads it.

Neil Duffy has shared the incredible story of a boy, Robbie Jones, who joins an ageless fraternity when he is presented with an ancient Native American lacrosse stick by Navy's Jimmy Lewis, considered by many, myself included, to be one of the game's greatest players. The stick and its original custodian, an Indian boy named Red Hawk, lead Robbie on a journey to places and times and to meetings with people he could never have imagined. Robbie learns lessons of integrity, respect, and honor from each of the stick's previous custodians.

This story is a major contribution to the great game of lacrosse. Indeed, it *transcends* the game. The rich historical and spiritual roots of its main characters provide stories which will touch every reader, regardless of age, gender, or association with the game of lacrosse.

In much the way lacrosse does, *The Spirit in the Stick* will captivate your heart, mind, and soul. It will get into *your* blood. Prepare to embark on a marvelous and special journey. I'm sure you will enjoy it!

Bob Scott
Johns Hopkins University
April 2004

# Preface

This project began some thirteen years ago, with a relatively benign phone call from Tom Duquette to me. Tom was coaching the lacrosse team at Norfolk Academy, and I held a corresponding position at nearby Nansemond-Suffolk Academy. At that point I had known Tom for several years. In fact, he was instrumental in encouraging and supporting my pursuing a career in education.

Over the years we had discussed a variety of topics related to lacrosse and other sports as well as education in general. When we discussed the history of the game of lacrosse, Tom always spoke reverently of Jimmy Lewis, United States Naval Academy Class of 1966, placing him on the same rung with his childhood heroes Johnny Unitas and Brooks Robinson. Lewis had a tremendous impact on Tom as a young lacrosse player growing up in Baltimore. Though I had played lacrosse at Navy myself, I was embarrassed to realize that my knowledge of Captain Lewis's career was close to non-existent. I had, thankfully, known *of* him, but I did not fully understand his on-field brilliance or that of his team, his true place in the history of Navy Lacrosse, or in the history of the game.

The nature of Tom's call was simple enough: Could you contact the Naval Academy and get a video tape of Jimmy Lewis? Tom had hoped to share the video with his players, one in particular who had developed a burning desire to study all the great attackmen in history. As with all things, actual video would be more valuable than a second-hand description of Lewis's play or an attempt to replicate it. I thought it a simple enough request, one upon which I might be able to exercise some sort of alumni privilege. And surely the Naval Academy had tape of their teams and players of that era, including Lewis.

It didn't take me long to realize that my search was not to be as simple as I had hoped or expected. After calling several offices at USNA, I was told that there were no such tapes, or at least none that anyone would be able to find. In disbelief, I began to call other schools Navy had played—Johns Hopkins, Army, Maryland—and other institutions, all to no avail. After several attempts (and a couple of years) to resurrect the tapes, I went straight to the source: Captain Lewis himself. No joy. More months. More years. Still nothing.

It became clear that I needed a new angle on this problem. So, in lieu of actual footage, I began to research Lewis's career, as well as the history of the game, so that I might find something useful for Tom and, at that point, *our* players (I had changed positions and was now working with Tom) at Norfolk Academy. As I dug further and further into the career of Captain James Crawford Lewis, U.S. Navy (Retired) and contacted a number of wonderful and helpful people, a remarkable story began to unfold before my eyes, leading me on a journey I never could have imagined.

Though this story's foundation is cast in the actual lives of its main characters, Major R. Bruce Turnbull, U.S. Army (Retired) and Captain Lewis granted me the necessary writer's license to connect the key elements of the story. Perhaps it is best left to the reader to decipher fact from fiction.

N.V.D.
Virginia Beach, VA
April 24, 2004

# Prologue

*If I had known that Jackson would drive us from our homes I would have
killed him that day at the Horseshoe.*
—Junaluska
Cherokee chief

Cherokee Territory: November 1, 1838

It was a typical fall morning in the Great Smoky
Mountains—cool and damp, with slate-colored clouds
hanging low in the sky. It seemed all-too-fitting that the rain
couldn't decide whether to fall or sit suspended, so it hung
motionless and heavy in the air. As a bugle commanded
"Forward, March," the notes ripped through the misty hearts
of the natives as surely and harshly as they did through the
misty air. While the Indians didn't know exactly what the
bugle call meant, their feet acknowledged that it probably
meant to move out. And so the wagons creaked into motion,
and hundreds of feet began to drag westward. Thus began
the infamous Trail of Tears, the forced migration of the
Cherokee Nation—and that of other Native Americans—
from their native homeland for relocation in the Indian
Territory to the west.

The lifeless bodies of the natives shuffled forward in the
mist, their goods, livestock, homes, clothes, blankets, and
children having been dispassionately and, in many cases,
violently stripped from them during the round-up weeks
earlier. Their strength, health, and spirit had been further

assaulted by the rancid conditions of the United States Army's holding pens.

A young brave, a seventeen-year-old named Red Hawk, clutched in his right hand a deerskin bag strapped across his chest, tilted his chin slightly skyward, and whispered, "Stay with me." His left hand held the trembling right hand of his eleven-year-old sister, Sunflower. In response to the bugle call, Red Hawk and Sunflower inched forward, hoping their movement might stir the feet of their father, Great Moose, who stood stoically, unable to look in the direction of the forced migration. He stood with his back facing south, a deliberate act of defiance signifying his contempt for Andrew Jackson.

Great Moose faced north, toward the land of his birth in the Great Smoky Mountains, where his wife had been buried two weeks earlier after being ravaged by cholera in the army stockade. Because in the time since he had eaten and drunk next to nothing, he was extremely weak. His heart had been shattered first by President Jackson, then by the soldiers during the round-up, and finally by the loss of his wife. He could bear no more.

Red Hawk released his sister's hand, and with a nod and a gentle nudge sent her to retrieve their father. The girl slid her hand into her father's and squeezed and tugged it ever so softly. Instinctively, her father, returning her unspoken love, turned slowly to her, and looked down into her beautiful brown eyes—mirrors of her mother's. Seeing his wife's face in place of his daughter's, he found his reason to go on, and looked to the north one last time to honor her memory. He turned back to the girl, this time he looked *through* her eyes and into her soul. Complying with her unspoken plea, he stepped with her toward the land of the setting sun.

Understanding, if not entirely empathizing with the unspeakable affront the bugle call had sealed upon the natives, the soldiers, at least for now, were more tolerant of

sluggish feet than they had been when they originally drove
the helpless victims to the pens, and allowed them to set their
own pace. As Red Hawk moved slowly ahead of his father
and sister, a young army officer guided his mount quietly
into the view of the young warrior, allowing the boy the
opportunity to make eye contact. Immediately Red Hawk
recognized the man as the officer who had overridden the
orders of two soldiers who had detained him as his mother
was being dragged from the stockade for burial.

Of the dozen-or-so Cherokee who had perished in the
stockade, only the family of the first to die, an old woman,
had been able to leave the pen to render appropriate burial
honors. Immediately after that burial, as the family made
their way back under the guard of two army privates, three
young men in the group broke and ran to hide in the hills.
After a short and fruitless chase, the soldiers summarily beat
the remaining family members and returned them to the
stockade. All future mourners attempting to accompany their
deceased loved ones were systematically thwarted by the
guards with their bayonets, which they did not hesitate to
use. The act of defiance of the three escapees had immediately
and unequivocally established future policy.

Red Hawk had clung to his mother's body as it was being
dragged by two army privates toward the camp gate, while
Sunflower cried as she watched from the arms of her mother's
brother. When Red Hawk encountered resistance in the form
of the bayonet, he had pleaded as best he could, "We will
bury her! We will bury her!" True to their orders, however, the
soldiers would have none of his defiance and had pushed
Red Hawk and his father roughly away from his mother's
corpse. Just as the boy had abandoned any hope of a proper
burial, an officer quietly approached on horseback from
outside the gate. While no words were spoken, the officer
immediately accepted the plea in the boy's eyes, a silent

promise guaranteeing he would not run if permitted to bury his mother.

The officer, who didn't seem much older than Red Hawk, intentionally allowed the sheath of his sword to clang against the heel of his boot, thus alerting the gate guards that an officer had just arrived; thereby eliciting a salute. The officer gently but firmly modified the standing order, "Let them take her. I will see to the situation."

"Yes, sir, lieutenant," one of the soldiers drawled for effect, "If you say so," and waved Red Hawk and Great Moose on with his rifle.

Red Hawk had carried his mother to the top of a nearby hill, and he began to dig her grave while his father stood and wept silently, his mind returning to Horseshoe Bend. For some three or four hours the lieutenant milled about on his mount a respectful distance away while Red Hawk and his father buried and prayed for his mother. Good to his unspoken pledge, Red Hawk escorted his grief-stricken father back to the stockade under the distant but trusting eye of the young lieutenant.

After the brief and silent exchange, the officer swung his horse with a snap on its bridle, thus departing as quietly and quickly as he had arrived not ten seconds before. Red Hawk and his family continued on their weary way.

*History is the mighty tower of experience, which time has built amidst the endless fields of bygone ages. It is no easy task to reach the top of this ancient structure and get the benefit of the full view. There is no elevator, but young feet are strong and it can be done.*
—Hendrik Willem van Loon
*The Story of Mankind*

# The Spirit in the Stick

# Past Meets Future

*The past opens the door to the future.*
—Class of 1910 Gate
Navy-Marine Corps Memorial Stadium
Annapolis, Maryland

Jim Lewis watched and waited patiently for the game to end as a lifetime of memories swirled around in his head. Rather than subject itself to such unfamiliar anarchy, his brain systematically quelled the maelstrom by organizing the whirl of thoughts into small, short snippets of a blessed life. His experienced fighter-pilot eyes tracked his target, an intrepid young lacrosse player—a ninth-grader, he guessed—finishing his game. Unbeknownst to him or anyone besides Lewis, the boy had been in radar-lock for two weeks now. The boy's life was about to change, for the better Lewis hoped, as his own had nearly a half-century earlier.

Though Lewis knew this moment would come, he didn't completely know what to expect, but in typical fashion he dealt with this watershed event like all others in his life—calmly, dispassionately, and by-the-book. He was acutely aware of all things happening both within him and without. He felt the emotion. He felt the years of memories run like a torrent through his mind but somehow was able to absorb them as they flooded by. He felt the significance of what was about to happen as well as a longing to go back and do it all again. He also felt a sense of relief at having met a lifetime of arduous challenges with grace and dignity. Now it was time.

Lewis waited for the post-game cheers and handshakes and then strode slowly, but purposefully, toward the young man and his parents. When it was clear to the parents that the stranger wished to speak with them, they slowed and offered inquisitive looks. They had never met this man. The stranger was nondescript in his appearance, of average height, perhaps five-eight or -nine. He was wearing duck boots, khakis, a blue golf jacket, dark sunglasses, and a plain blue ball cap. The salt-and-pepper hair beneath the cap betrayed some age, but otherwise his thin, strong, athletic frame could have easily deceived the couple into thinking he was a man twenty years younger. Before he spoke, he presented a remarkably digni-fied appearance.

"Good afternoon. My name is Jim Lewis," he said as he extended his hand.

They introduced themselves as Mary and John Jones and then introduced their daughter Catherine. The boy firmly shook the stranger's hand, "I'm Robbie."

Lewis asked if the family had a few minutes to chat about lacrosse and, more importantly, about Robbie. He wanted to talk now—timing was important—and, if at all possible, on this field. Though a little confused and skeptical, the parents graciously indulged him.

"When I was about Robbie's age, I was presented a lacrosse stick—a very special lacrosse stick—by a complete stranger, as I am to you right now. I have had the stick for about forty-two years, and it has meant a great deal to me," Lewis began. "The man who gave me the stick, Mr. Doug Turnbull, made only two requests of me. The first was to do my best to respect the game of lacrosse and the second was to pass the stick along to a worthy young man who might also put it to good use. I played lacrosse quite a few years ago and did my best to respect the game and its history. And now it is time to pass it along. I would like Robbie to have it."

Lewis failed to mention that he had not just played the game, but had *revolutionized* it in the nineteen-sixties during a string of national championship teams at the United States Naval Academy. And he didn't mention a distinguished career as a naval aviator—twenty-nine years as a fighter- and test-pilot.

Lewis walked the family to the trunk of his car, where he carefully pulled out an old leather bag by its shoulder strap, the contents secured by leather thongs. It was an unusual and unique arrangement, not something you would expect to hold a lacrosse stick. He carefully untied the thongs, slipped the stick out, and handed it to the boy.

"Robbie, this stick is over 200 years old, and it has a remarkable history and some special qualities that I would like to share with you."

When Lewis placed the stick in his hand the boy felt his whole body tingle. It felt perfectly balanced and at home in his hands.

Lewis continued, "The stick has managed to survive as it has been passed down through several generations during those two hundred years. It is perhaps the oldest lacrosse stick still in use. The men who had it before me took very good care of it, and I've tried to do my part."

As Robbie held the stick Lewis softly touched the leather and gut netting inside the head of the stick, the pocket. "This is the soul of the stick, Robbie," Lewis said, gazing softly at the net and gently caressing the strings.

The boy and the parents could see that Lewis's fingers had traveled these strings countless times before. He continued, "The true essence of a stick is its pocket. The person who crafted this stick did so with the care, wisdom, passion, and precision of an Indian warrior. Look at the strings, the knots, the alignment of them in relation to each other, and all the care that was put into the stringing. The warrior spirit has been passed down through these strings. You see, the bent branch is what gives this stick its shape, but the true character of the stick is embedded in these strings. Here, touch them. You can feel the oil and imagine the sweat from the hands of the warriors who used it."

Robbie began to trace the strings with his fingers.

"The wood has been oiled and plied meticulously over the years. Take a look at the engravings on the shaft. Those were carved by each of the previous custodians."

Robbie immediately began to wonder what those unusual carvings meant but was too overwhelmed to ask. He wrapped his left hand around the butt end of the shaft, holding it in its normal grip. Just above his hand was the first of a series of horizontal rings, each pair flanking a carving. As Robbie studied the hieroglyphics from bottom to top, his mind raced. The bottom figure looked like an Indian woman with arms outstretched. The next looked like a bird of prey, its beak and talons clearly defined. Above the next ring was a magnificently carved flower, a sunflower, Robbie thought. The boy was struck by the detail and care of the carving. The next figure on the shaft looked to be a place of worship, a church or chapel. Above the chapel was inscribed a flattened out cross. Moving up, Robbie's fingers traced the outline of what looked like the Olympic Rings. They, too, were carved with particular care. Perhaps one of the previous custodians had been an Olympian, Robbie thought. Next on the shaft was a carving of a book, with a barely visible title inscribed upon its cover. The final picture was clearly the block letter "N" with a small group of stars clustered above its upper right corner. Interestingly, on each shank of the "N" there seemed to be the outline of maps. One had the rough appearance of the letter "J" or a fishhook, the other a long slender figure that forked toward its end.

Robbie then traced out letters arranged along the shaft and wrapping around the head of the stick itself. The boy was mystified that they were not from his language, or at least he didn't think they were. The letters, he guessed, were some sort of sentence or phrase. What did it say? What did it mean? Who had written it?

Lewis brought Robbie back to the discussion, "The stick is in great shape. It is from an ancient Iroquois chief who probably crafted it around the year 1780. The sticks of the Iroquois are the forerunners of the modern stick we use today. "I won't go through the entire history of the stick now, for that history will become more clear over time. My only requests are the same ones passed to me: Please respect the game and pass this stick along to another when the time comes."

The parents were completely stunned and confused. The mother was only able to question, "Why Robbie? Why now?"

"I'm an avid fan of the game with a special interest in unique talent. Robbie plays lacrosse as it should be played. I've been looking for a young player who displays the ancient essence of the game. Why? That will become clear as I explain a few things."

Robbie and his parents looked at one another, wondering where this stranger was going with this rather peculiar start. "This stick was crafted in a time when Indian warriors played the game. It was part of a culture, and their tradition required that the stick be passed down among warriors, players who learned how, when, and where to be hunters, players who could rely on their patience and then strike at the right time. I've seen your son display those traits. I also feel that true lacrosse players should play with enthusiasm, class, physical and mental toughness, and team spirit. The game, after all, was and is a team game. I've been looking for a young warrior with character, spirit, and leadership but, mainly, for a player who puts his team ahead of himself. When Mr. Turnbull presented the stick to me that was one of the things he talked about. He always said that no matter how talented someone might be, he was always obliged to contribute his efforts to the higher good—the team. Mr. Turnbull said he learned that lesson through lacrosse, and it applied to everything he did in his life. 'With talent and ability,' he would say, 'comes responsibility.' My high school coach used to tell me much the same thing: 'Those to whom much is given, much is expected.'"

The lives of the Joneses—and Lewis—had changed quite a bit in the last fifteen minutes.

"This is a bit overwhelming for us. I hope you understand," the father conceded.

"I do."

Lewis asked Robbie if he could borrow his game stick and then asked him to go about twenty yards away so they could throw and catch. The boy sprinted to the appointed spot to make his first throw with the stick. He saw the target that Lewis held up. He was focused on a spot in the pocket of Lewis's stick about the size of a quarter. He could clearly see the intersection of the center raw-hide string in the pocket with the center of the supporting gut cross webbing. At the same time he could see his parents moving to his right and other members of his team with their parents leaving the field on the left. What was going on? He made his first pass. Lewis didn't move the target an inch. The sound of the ball in the netting, on target, straight and true as an arrow. Robbie thought, WOW! This stick is two hundred years old! He had never held an "old time" stick like this or thrown such a perfect pass. Robbie studied the stick. He could feel its natural and inherent balance. Visually, the stick seemed to lack the symmetry of his high-tech, latest model year attack stick. But when his eyes focused on his new playing partner, he felt something special in his hands. He had never experienced this feeling before, a feeling that old-timers considered a bond with their sticks. Today's mass-produced "cookie cutter" sticks were all manufactured in exactly the same way, bought off the shelf with little thought or care and discarded just as easily. Robbie and his peers would never have guessed that the hand-crafted wooden sticks had a feel, a balance, a weight, and a character—a personality—of their own. A player in Lewis's era and earlier might lift hundreds of sticks, one at a time, off warehouse racks, twirl and fiddle with each one until he found the stick that felt just right. His stick became part of him. Sometimes, if a player were truly fortunate, he would find a special stick that provided instant feedback and acceptance.

As Robbie threw and caught with the stranger, he could still feel his body, particularly his hands, tingling. It had felt this way for almost thirty minutes, since he first touched the stick. Maybe it was the fact that a stranger thought so highly of his play. Maybe it was the fact that he was holding a 200-year-old lacrosse stick. Never mind, he thought. This is really cool. Enjoy it for now.

After throwing for a few more minutes, Lewis asked the boy to stand fast. He reached further into the leather bag and withdrew an old lacrosse ball. It was a sphere about the same size as today's rubber ball—perhaps a little bigger—but it was clearly made of some sort of hide and sewn tight with sinew. Lewis first showed it to the boy.

"This is a lot more delicate than that stick, so we'll just take a few throws with it, O.K.?" The boy's eyes got even bigger.

"You'd be amazed at what is inside this skin," Lewis teased. "All sorts of things like rocks, feathers, worms, and pieces of bat wings."

The parents' eyes began to light up as well. "You're kidding?" said Robbie's father, while his daughter looked on in equal amazement.

"Not at all. The Native Americans would sew certain things into the ball to make it more lively and to increase their chances of winning."

They took a dozen or so throws, being a little more gentle with this gem. Robbie could not believe how the deerskin ball flew out of his stick. It had such a natural feel to it. His hands still tingled. Lewis took the ball from his stick and placed it back in the leather bag.

"Whenever you're not using this stick, you should place this hide ball in the stick—exactly where the pocket is. Be attentive to where you place this ball. Remember that the pocket is the soul of the stick," Lewis instructed as he put the rubber ball back in his stick and began to throw again.

Lewis continued to throw with the boy, pausing a few seconds here and there to crystallize a thought or make a point, but hardly skipping a beat. Lewis delivered perfect right-handed and left-handed passes each time, right to the boy's "ear," just where Robbie's coaches preached they should be. The boy did not reciprocate the changing of hands with Lewis, fearful that his comparative lack of skill on his left side might cause him to miss or drop an incoming strike or throw an errant pass. Lewis hoped the boy would change hands as he did but was not surprised that he didn't. When the boy continued with his right hand, Lewis gently chided, "Try it with your left hand." Robbie immediately obliged. He felt the stick throw slightly differently from the left side, and it took him several throws to acclimate to the change.

The boy was already beginning to feel the power of the stick. The fact that it was made from a tree branch, Robbie thought, may have contributed to the way it felt. He had always used an aluminum- or titanium-shafted stick, with its cold, factory-produced, inert feeling. This wooden stick almost felt *alive*! But it couldn't be alive, he convinced himself.

As they threw Lewis watched Robbie carefully. He could see the boy glancing at the stick, and then at his hands, in disbelief. The retired captain also knew what the boy was feeling. His hands had tingled in the same way since 1959. Lewis allowed himself a hint of a smile as he continued to watch the boy.

Lewis then paused and again reaching into the bag, pulled out an old wooden jewelry box. He opened it and withdrew three books, a very old copy of *Uncle Tom's Cabin, Het*

*Achterhuis* (*The Diary of Anne Frank*), and *The Story of Mankind.*
Lewis offered, "The first two were passed along to me with the
stick. The third one I am adding to the stick's legacy. The
*Uncle Tom's Cabin* is an original edition, signed by the author.
You'll learn of the significance of these books as you go along."
Lewis placed the books gently back in the box, closed the
cover, and handed it to Robbie.

Lewis handed the parents his business card. "I live and
work in California, but I'm in town on business this week."

Robbie's parents, still overwhelmed and confused, politely
said, "How can we thank you? Will we meet again?"

"That's entirely up to you. I'd be glad to further the relationship, but I won't impose anything on you or Robbie. The
stick will take care of itself. If you never see me again, I'm
certain that Robbie will benefit from being its custodian. I've
done what I was asked to do."

They all began to walk toward the family's car, along an
asphalt path adorned by a two-foot-high brick wall that
followed the tree line of the adjacent woods. As always, Lewis's
keen senses made him acutely aware of the sights, sounds,
and smells of his surroundings. As they approached a section
of the wall nearest the overhanging trees, Lewis suddenly
asked the boy to hand him the stick and a ball. He gestured
toward the wall and, in a whisper, asked them if they could
see a small bird on the edge of the path trying to fly. It had
probably just fallen out of a nest in the tree above but they
hadn't noticed until Lewis brought it to their attention. Lewis
then pointed out a long black snake about twelve feet away
from the bird, making its way through a crack in the brick-
work toward the helpless bird. They immediately calculated
the imminent peril of the young bird.

Lewis positioned himself and drew the stick much like
an archer would hold a bow prior to raising it up and arming
the arrow. In something of a trance he said softly to them, but
really to himself, "Every creature should be given the oppor-

tunity to succeed, the chance to spread its wings and reach its potential."

The ball left the stick like a laser toward the snake and hit the wall twelve inches in front of its head, exactly where Lewis intended. There was no reason to hit the snake. The serpent recoiled but quickly pressed on. Lewis fired three more shots, each one progressively closer to the snake, until it turned back.

Realizing that the bird would fall prey to the same or some other predator as soon as they left, the family scooped up the bird, and Robbie placed it back in its nest. They all stared at Lewis, who paused for some time and then said matter-of-factly, "You see, this stick has helped me acquire that same focus and keen awareness of the warriors before me. It has helped me channel that focus into just about everything I've done. It is not just the senses required for success on the playing field but also in meeting the challenges of my chosen path through life—warfare in the ancient sense. It has made me sensitive to so many things in my daily life, my family, and my job. I simply don't take anything for granted— not a single life, a single person, or a single heartbeat. This stick has been very special to me. Of the many lessons I've learned from the stick, one is that the gift of life is both precious and precarious."

Arriving at the Jones's car, the new friends shook hands, and Lewis handed the bag, stick, and ball back to the boy. He thanked the parents for allowing him to present the stick and books to Robbie and then began to walk back down the path.

As Lewis found himself below the nest of the bird, he lingered, thinking that the entire transaction had not been nearly as difficult as he thought it would be. What an incredible coincidence that he was able to use the stick to spare the life of the bird. Well, it wasn't really a coincidence, he suspected. Just then, a warm, swift current of air swept by him and rustled the leaves above. Lewis was familiar with the signal. He looked up toward the nest and whispered, "Good-bye, my good friend. I've done what has been asked. I hope that I have rendered sufficient honor to you, your people, and your game. I hope that Robbie will be as blessed as I have been."

Lewis continued along the path, blinking back a tear or two. Then he began to glow a little inside. The joy in the boy's eyes and the stunned looks of the parents spoke volumes of the impact he had had on the boy. Lewis wondered how Robbie would do and how long it would take for the stick to reveal its true character to him. His eye caught the leading edge of the full moon as it rose above the trees in the distance. He smiled and whispered to himself, "Not long, not long."

# A Visit from Red Hawk

*To penetrate the Indian game, one must enter a world of
spiritual belief and magic.*
—Dr. Thomas Vennum, Jr.
*American Indian Lacrosse: Little Brother of War*

Robbie was too excited to sleep that night. He tossed for
hours, staring out his window at the light from the full moon
and dreaming of the endless possibilities of the stick. His
imagination spun questions and answers concerning the carvings and writing on the shaft. Finally, after drifting off, he
was met in a dream by a young Indian boy. Though asleep to
the rest of the world, Robbie was completely awake in his
dream, fully aware of what was happening to him.

*The Indian boy approached Robbie and introduced himself.
"Hello, I'm Red Hawk. You're Robbie, right?"*

*"Yes," Robbie said, stunned that the stranger knew his name.*

*"And you are now the custodian of the stick?" Red Hawk asked
with a broad smile.*

*Robbie smiled back, "Mr. Lewis gave me the stick this after-
noon."*

*"Well, it's nice to meet you," Red Hawk offered sincerely.*

*"Same here," gushed Robbie, overwhelmed by the notion that
he might be talking to someone who had lived two-hundred years
before. Though Robbie didn't ask, based on their similar heights he
could tell that Red Hawk was about his age, perhaps fourteen.*

*"When he gave me the stick, Mr. Lewis told me that it was*

special, but I had no idea that this is what he meant." Robbie continued. "This is unbelievable!"

"Well, I know this is hard for you to believe, but through the stick I have been able to visit several other boys, and all of them had the same initial response. They have all been great boys and men!"

"What am I supposed to do with the stick?" Robbie posed as an obvious first question.

"That's up to you. You can do whatever you want," Red Hawk smiled again.

Robbie wasn't sure what was in the realm of possibility, so he asked a more pointed question. "Mr. Lewis told me that I would be able to find out more about the history of this stick through the stick itself. Did he mean that someone like you would be able to teach me things?"

"That depends on what you want to learn," Red Hawk replied cryptically.

"Can you tell me how you got the stick, then?"

"Sure. But perhaps we should talk about some other things first. I should start by saying, Robbie, that we'll be able to visit people and places of the past. We'll be able to see and hear all around us, but none of the people of those earlier times will notice us. We'll be there, but we'll be completely unknown and invisible to anyone involved," Red Hawk explained.

Robbie's dream was so real and so clear and he went deeper into its magic.

Red Hawk thought it best to begin with a narrative on the nature of the game of lacrosse in his culture.

"For any young man in our Cherokee tribe, these sticks symbolized a great deal. As soon as we touched the sticks, every one of us could immediately feel the power and spirit of the warriors, living and deceased, in our tribe. What the French named lacrosse, we called stickball. The game was a central part of our lives as boys, a way for us to be accepted as men. When we were still too young to go into battle with our older brothers, uncles, and fathers, stick-

*ball substituted as a means to show our strength, skill, and courage—the same traits that would make us successful as hunters and defenders of our tribe. When we became older, we still played with passion, mostly to invite the favor of our gods, to strengthen our boys, to earn respect for our clans in contests with others, and to continue to parade our physical prowess and courage. It was a game but also a tool that helped us become men. Would you like to see what the game looked like for my people?"*

"Sure!"

Red Hawk walked Robbie through a small stand of shade trees which ran into the shadows and burst out into a bright, sun-lit meadow. This was Robbie's first trip through time and it was to a Cherokee village on the Little Tennessee River in current-day Smoky Mountain National Park on the western edge of North Carolina. The year was 1835.

Red Hawk began, "This is the clan of my grandfather, the Bear Clan. They are preparing for a stickball game with the Wolf Clan, who issued a challenge earlier in the summer."

Robbie soaked in the lush green scenery, the gentle mountains all around. Red Hawk led Robbie to a small stream where they saw about twenty Cherokee young men waist deep in the water. Red Hawk described the scene.

"These players are undergoing preparations for the contest tomorrow. They must cleanse themselves completely. Our tribe calls this ritual 'going to water.' It is conducted almost exactly like the ceremony for warriors going on the war path. It is necessary for each combatant, each player in this case, to cleanse and purge themselves."

Some of the youngest warriors drank strong spirits from a jug and immediately vomited in the stream.

"That man," Red Hawk pointed out the older man, "is the village conjurer or shaman. He is responsible for invoking the proper spirits and rituals to ensure success."

Robbie watched as the man wiped ointment on the small sticks and then prayed over them. The boy noticed the interesting shape *of the sticks. They were much smaller than he expected, and they were used in pairs. They were not quite like the one he had just inherited.*

*"The conjurers play a great role in determining the outcome of a contest," Red Hawk shared. "They perform many rituals over the players. They even cast spells on the opposing team to impose poor play on them."*

*The young men left the stream and began to march to the village center, where they were received by a large assemblage. "This is the ball play dance, Robbie. To energize their team all the villagers come out to offer chants, to beat drums, and to dance. These events will go on well into the night."*

*Red Hawk then took Robbie to the events of the next morning. They observed the players wearing only breechclouts around their waists and feathers in their hair, marching in single file with sticks in hand to the river. "They are going to water again, Robbie. Each player has fasted at least since yesterday. Now once more they will cleanse themselves."*

*The players dipped their sticks in the water and then bathed themselves. As the players waded out of the water, the conjurer 'scratched' each player. Robbie was shocked to observe the blood seeping out of the shallow gashes. Red Hawk brought Robbie closer. The boy stared at the scratching implement. It looked like a comb with about six or eight teeth. The teeth, however, were rattlesnake fangs inserted into a feather's quill. The shaman dipped the comb into a pot of sacred plant juice and meticulously etched the body of each warrior. Some of the players requested scratching in two or three areas—the chest, the arms, and the legs—with the hope that this would strengthen their lungs and limbs for the contest. After scratching, the conjurer rubbed all of the players with ointment.*

*The players then again formed a single file and began their march to the field in step with the beat of a war drum. Some of the players bellowed whoops as they marched. Most focused silently within themselves, invoking the Great Spirit to provide strength and courage.*

Before the contest started, the conjurers of each team escorted the players to the center of the field, where they faced each other. Robbie marveled at the similarity to the pre-game lineup of his games. The conjurers then offered instructions on the rules of the contest and on fair play. Robbie noticed the goals were about three hundred yards apart and marked by two sticks set about ten feet apart.

Play began with two center men battling for a ball tossed in the air. A face-off, Robbie thought. Play was intense. The ball was often picked up with one stick and then carried with the second stick placed on top of the first. It seemed as though the fastest, strongest, and smartest players were the most successful. Passing did not seem to be an integral part of the game—many players simply ran with the ball until they were stopped by force, resulting in a mad scramble for a loose ball. Robbie watched in amazement as several pairs of players dropped their sticks and wrestled each other.

Play went on for a few hours, the Bear Clan scoring fifteen goals to the Wolf's twelve. After the game, the players again adjourned to the river for cleansing and finally to the village center for the Victory Dance.

"You can see, Robbie, these ceremonies are as important as the games themselves. The Victory Dance is similar to the one we perform when warriors return from battle."

Robbie remembered that Red Hawk had said that his people were the Cherokee and Mr. Lewis had told him that the stick was from the Iroquois.

"Did you say that your people were the Cherokee?"

"Yes. Why do you ask?"

"Well, Mr. Lewis told my family and me that this stick was from the Iroquois."

"Oh, right. Well, we will have plenty of time to discuss that. I'll be back to see you soon. We must go now." He gestured to the shadows, and they quickly moved into the trees. "I really just wanted to introduce myself tonight. I'll see you again soon."

The next morning Robbie woke none the worse for having

been engaged in such a real and passionate dream. He shared the experience with his parents, who rather quickly dismissed it as a fantastical trip brought on by the excitement of the previous day.

# Classmates and Teammates

*I can't help but be grateful for all of the teams, coaches,
and teammates I have had in my athletic pursuits. Those people
and experiences have prepared me well for this position.
For war is a team sport every bit as much as lacrosse is.*
—From a letter by
LCOL John I. Turnbull to his mother,
October 18, 1944

Over the following days Robbie insisted to his parents that his dream was different—it was a visit. As the boy persisted, his parents' concern grew. Did Mr. Lewis know this would happen? Was this stick really that special? What could happen to Robbie?

They continued to caution Robbie that his dream was simply that—a dream—mostly because they were not able to understand, explain, or control such supernatural phenomena. The parents wanted to call Lewis, but they agreed to wait.

Robbie continued his assertions of a visit and, when his parents would not accept his reasoning, he accused them of not understanding him and belittling his thoughts. They finally relented and called Lewis in California, who was not surprised to hear from them.

"Mr. Lewis, this is John Jones, Robbie's father. You gave him the stick."

"Yes, Mr. Jones, good to hear from you."

"Would you mind if I put you on speaker phone with my

wife?"

"Not at all. Please do."

"Well, the reason we are calling is that Robbie has told us some interesting things that are somehow related to the stick, and we were hoping that you might be able to shed some light on his behavior."

"I'll be glad to try. What types of interesting things?" Lewis asked, knowing all too well what he was about to hear.

"Well, Robbie seems to think that he was *visited* by a young Indian named Red Hawk while he was sleeping. Robbie has told us that he has never experienced any dream like this. He said he was wide awake during it, that he knew exactly what was going on, and that he has total recall of every detail.

"It happened about three weeks ago—I believe it was the night that you gave him the stick. He has also mentioned a sort of tingling in his hands every time he touches the stick." The parents could not see Lewis smiling through the phone.

"Anything else?"

"That's really about it—do you know anything about this? You said that it was a special stick. Is this what you meant?"

"Well, you will probably find what I am about to say completely incredible, but please bear with me. While I was the custodian of that stick, I beheld similar visions, and many others have as well."

The parents felt a chill and looked at each other in disbelief. Was this some sort of spell? He should have told us about this. Was this possible? They maintained their composure and allowed Lewis to continue.

"Before you become too alarmed, I can assure you that no harm will come to your boy because of this stick."

"But you can understand our apprehension?"

"Of course I can. I know what Robbie is going through. I think we'll need to continue this discussion in person. I'll be in town this weekend. Would you mind waiting till then?"

"No, we can wait until then, but not longer, please."

"That would be great," Lewis responded.

"Can we say Saturday night at 7 for dinner?" Mary offered.

"Yes. I'll be there, but could you please do me a favor before then? If you are concerned about my credibility, please call the Superintendent at the United States Naval Academy, Admiral Ed Charles. He'll provide you an independent source on my background."

After they hung up Robbie's parents were even more uneasy.

First thing the next morning the Joneses called the Superintendent.

"Admiral Charles's office, may I help you?" said the friendly voice of a middle-aged woman.

"Y-Yes, my name is John Jones. May I speak to Admiral Charles, please?"

"Yes, Mr. Jones, the admiral was expecting your call."

"Good morning, Mr. Jones, this is Ed Charles. Captain Lewis told me to expect your call. What can I do for you?"

"Admiral, would you mind if I put my wife on the speakerphone?"

"Please."

"Well, admiral, we just met Mr. Lewis for the first time about a month ago, but he's suddenly become a big part of our lives. You see, he chose to make our son the recipient of a very old Native American lacrosse stick he had received many years ago. He said that it was really quite a remarkable gift and—well—it has been so overwhelming. Mr. Lewis asked me to call to ease some of our apprehension."

"I understand. So you need some confirmation of Captain Lewis's background, integrity, and so on?"

"Yes, sir, I suppose."

"Then you apparently know very little about Jim Lewis, is that right?"

"That's right."

"Well, let me start by saying that I've known Jim since we were plebes—that is, freshmen—here at the Naval Academy in 1962. We were Plebe Summer roommates, classmates, and teammates. That's almost forty years and counting. I can assure you, Mr. and Mrs. Jones that Jim is one of the finest people I've ever known. He's a truly great naval officer, leader, navy pilot, and person. Everything else I'll say is simply icing. You said Jim gave your son a lacrosse stick?"

"Yes."

"So I'll bet that Jim conveniently failed to share his lacrosse background with you?"

"That's right. Well, he did say that he had played many years ago and that it had been a big part of his life. I think that is all he said."

"Well, Jim has never been one to toot his own horn, so let me do it for him a little. Again, keep in mind at this point that none of this really matters because the lacrosse aspect of Jim's life only helped create the foundation for his future successes. He's been a leader all of the years that I've known him. But it might be good for you and your son to know that Jim is widely considered the greatest lacrosse player ever. When he was at the Naval Academy he revolutionized the way the game was played.

"If you talk to many lacrosse people about the players who dominated the game over the years, most would single out Jim. Paul and Gary Gait of Syracuse University, Mark Millon of the University of Massachusetts, and one or two others have certainly achieved greatness in the modern era. But the game is different now. Back when Jim played, no one had seen anyone like him. Prior to Jim, I guess you'd have to mention Jim Brown—also of Syracuse—Class of '57. If you're wondering, yes, he is the Jim Brown of football fame. He was a tremendous lacrosse player also. It is difficult to compare any of these players directly since they were all so fantastic. But it is fair to consider Jim in a class of his own. He was inducted into the National Lacrosse Hall-of-Fame in 1982."

The Joneses stared at each other in disbelief.

"Jim and I played together for all four years here. Our first year was on the plebe team. Then we won three straight national championships, and our record was something like 35-1. Not many people know or believe this, but in 1963 our plebe team defeated our varsity in a pretty formal scrimmage. Under most circumstances that would be impressive but, in this case, that varsity team won the *national championship*! We love to ride those guys about that, and we continue to do so after all these years. We had several excellent players and coaches, but Jim was central to our success. He was a phenomenal player. Jim was first-team All-America and received the Turnbull Award three consecutive years."

"The Turnbull Award?" the father asked, recognizing the name that Lewis had mentioned when they first met.

"Oh, forgive me. That's the award given annually to the top attackman in lacrosse. Division I players back then, and nowadays in Division II and Division III, I believe."

The parents remained speechless.

"Hello…?" the admiral inquired as he heard the silence.

"Y-Yes, we're still here," the father offered.

"Should I continue?"

"Please do."

"Well, in 1991 Jim was honored by the NCAA with their Silver Anniversary Award. Jim's high school background is probably worth noting as well. On Long Island, Jim was a member of a team that came out of nowhere and won many lacrosse championships. When he graduated, he was considered a unique lacrosse player. He played at a level that no one was familiar with. He was playing the game in a different way and with remarkable results. He once scored ten goals and had eleven assists in less than *half* of one game. He also collected a number of very prestigious awards. By the time he left Long Island his reputation as a player was spreading to the major centers of lacrosse. Recently, he was the first name mentioned for a mythical All-Century team. Should I go on?"

"Please, if you don't mind."

"Well, from there Jim went on to become a top-notch naval aviator and test pilot. He was a superb pilot and naval officer."

The Joneses didn't want to ask the next question, but the mother could not hold back, "Did Mr. Lewis ever mention anything about the old Native American stick that he had?"

"I know he kept an old stick in a leather bag. But he never talked about it or used it when anyone was around. He was pretty protective of it. I'd be a little surprised that he gave that stick away. I wonder if that is the one he passed to your son."

"I think it probably is," said the father.

"Well, that is very interesting. I never knew much about his stick, but I did know at the time when we were room-mates that the stick contributed to his fascination with the game and its ancient history. I'm sure that his knowledge of the game's history accentuated his magnificent skills. He studied every aspect of the game. He loved—and thrived on—the game's ancient roots and often referred to its warrior nature.

"What else can I help you with?"

"Nothing, you've been very helpful. Oh, how should we address him?"

"Jim retired as a captain, but he would probably wish to be called just Jim. If you insist on being formal, he is tech-nically Captain Lewis."

"Thank you very much, admiral. We can't tell you how much we appreciate this."

"You're quite welcome. Please let me know if I may be of further assistance. Good luck."

"Thank you again, admiral. Good bye."

The parents stared at each other again. They intentionally did not share the contents of this discussion with Robbie and began to make preparations for Lewis's visit.

# Simply Phenomenal

Robbie stared at the stick as it sat against his bedroom wall with the leather-covered ball placed in the pocket as Lewis had instructed. Much to Robbie's disappointment, for twenty-eight days Red Hawk had not appeared to him. The boy had not calculated the actual interval, noting only that it seemed interminably long. He drifted off to sleep, despairing that he might not see Red Hawk again and that the first visit, as his parents suggested, had just been a creation of his mind. But as the clouds rose in the sky, unveiling a full moon, Red Hawk finally came to Robbie.

*"Hi, Robbie!" Red Hawk offered enthusiastically.*

*"Hi! I was wondering if you were ever coming back. The last few days I wasn't sure if we had really met."*

*"We met, that's for sure. Do you want to take another trip?"*

*"Sure! Where are we going?"*

*"Would you like to learn a little bit about Captain Lewis?"*

*"Yes!" Robbie gushed.*

*Red Hawk took Robbie to Navy-Marine Corps Memorial Stadium in Annapolis, Maryland, May 1, 1982, for the game between Johns Hopkins University and Navy.*

*"This is a very special stadium, Robbie."*

*Robbie nodded as he scanned the facades of the stadium containing names of battles and campaigns in which USNA graduates had fought. He recognized at least two, IWO JIMA and PEARL HARBOR, and surmised that the other thirty or forty names carried similar significance.*

*Red Hawk brought Robbie near the Navy sideline. Shortly after their arrival, both teams departed the field for half-time. Red Hawk pointed out the ceremony about to begin. A group of people, led by a very tall man, strode several yards onto the field to a microphone that had just been placed there by a maintenance worker. The group included the tall man, retired navy captain J.O. Coppedge, the current athletic director at the Naval Academy; a much shorter man, Willis P. Bilderback, former coach of the midshipmen lacrosse team; a young midshipman escorting the official party, and a commander with his wife and two small children.*

*Captain Coppedge took the microphone.*

*"Ladies and gentlemen, it is with great pleasure that I welcome you to the induction ceremony for our own Commander Jimmy Lewis '66 into the National Lacrosse Hall-of-Fame. Tradition has it that the presenter of an inductee has the privilege of offering remarks to the assemblage. Because of his failing voice Coach Bilderback has asked me to offer comments, and I have gladly accepted such a high honor. We thank you for being here to share this special moment with Jim, his family, and, of course, his great coach, Willis Bilderback.*

*"I was extremely fortunate to have seen nearly every game that Jim played for three national championship teams here at the Naval Academy–1964, '65, and '66. It would be impossible to share all of Jim's countless accomplishments with you. We'll have time to mention only a few.*

*"Jim's play and leadership were simply phenomenal. He was quick, tough, smart, and an unbelievable competitor. He had a self-confidence—I don't mind saying that some of our opponents*

*might call it cockiness—about himself that made his team better. He simply felt and played as though he and his team could beat anybody.*

*"He single-handedly redefined the way attackmen played the game. Prior to Jim, attackmen were content to run around behind the goal and feed to teammates. Jim became the first attackman to really attack the cage, mostly by carrying the stick in one hand and tucking it behind his shoulder. All offensive players do it today in large part because the sticks are much smaller and lighter. Most young players today would never know how that stick position evolved. For three consecutive years Jim received the Turnbull Award as the country's top attackman, the only one who has ever accomplished such a feat. I'm one of the many people who believe that Jim deserved that Award his freshman year as well, but he was required to play on our plebe team because NCAA regulations prohibited freshmen from playing on the varsity.*

*"Jim was also a standout soccer player here even though he never played the game in high school. He scored the game-winning goal in the 1964 NCAA championship game when he was a junior. It is hard to imagine many athletes who have won national championships in two different sports and who played such keys roles for each!*

*"At graduation Jim was presented with the Naval Academy Athletic Sword. Some of you may remember that Roger Staubach had received the Award the year before. As a lacrosse player, Jim enjoyed the highest accolades from players, coaches, fans, journalists, and everyone else involved in the game. Many believe him to be the greatest player ever.*

*"Let me conclude by saying that Jim has forever changed the game of lacrosse and will be remembered by all Navy players and fans as the greatest ever. But beyond all of his phenomenal exploits on the field, he has achieved equal status as a navy pilot, a naval officer, and the leader of young men.*

*"Now please allow me to introduce Coach Willis Bilderback to present Jim for formal induction into the Hall of Fame."*

Coach Bilderback moved slowly to the microphone, the midshipman escort accompanying him with a large plaque.

"Jim, words cannot sum up what you have meant to your teammates, your coaches, your school, your family, and the great game of lacrosse. Thank you for letting us be a part of your life."

As his coach spoke Lewis stood with his head canted down, as if observing an invocation, then stood bolt upright and proceeded to the microphone.

"Captain Coppedge, thank you for your kind remarks. Coach, thank you for all that you've done for Navy Lacrosse, for our teams, and for me. Ladies and gentlemen, thank you for your kind attention and warm welcome.

"Since lacrosse is, above all, a team game, it makes me uncomfortable to be recognized for individual play. I never played the game of lacrosse for awards. I played it because it is simply a great and fun game to play. The game represents so much, mostly the physical, mental, and emotional challenges that it imposes on players and teams to do their best. It's a game with great history whose roots are grounded in the ancient Native American culture and whose fundamental use, in addition to its recreational value, was to prepare young warriors for battle. The game has been a true gift to me as it has allowed me to be a part of that culture.

"I could never have enjoyed any success in this game without the support and care of my teammates and coaches, particularly Coach Bilderback and Coach MacDonald of Uniondale High School, my family, and a very special guest, Mr. Doug Turnbull, Johns Hopkins, Class of 1924. Thank you."

Robbie followed Lewis's eyes into the first row of the stands, where Turnbull offered a modest wave to Lewis. The boy gazed at Turnbull in amazement, connecting the name Lewis had shared with the actual person.

Red Hawk and Robbie stayed for the second half of the game, watching Hopkins dampen Lewis's ceremony with a 12-7 victory. It was the first time Robbie had seen a college game.

"How would you like to see one of Captain Lewis's games,

Robbie?" Red Hawk asked.

"Sure—is it possible?"

Red Hawk took Robbie to Michie Stadium, West Point, New York for the 1964 Army-Navy game. Red Hawk explained that both teams came into the game undefeated and that the National Championship was now on the line. He pointed out the huge crowd of over 7,000—the largest ever at Michie Stadium for a lacrosse game. He told Robbie that the game was about half-way through the third quarter and pointed to the scoreboard which indicated that Navy was ahead 4-3.

"That's Captain Lewis, number 22," Red Hawk said, allowing Robbie to follow his eyes to the sophomore attackman. "This is his first Army-Navy game. He scored a goal in the first half when Navy had a two-man advantage to put them up 4-1. Army scored late in the first half to make it 4-2 and again a couple of minutes ago to make it 4-3. That has given them some much-needed confidence. Army's All-American goalkeeper, Norm Webb, has been fantastic the entire season. They are an excellent team and have held some very good teams like Maryland, Johns Hopkins, and Syracuse to under four goals per game. So let's see what happens."

Red Hawk allowed the scene to unfold with no further comment.

A few seconds later Lewis slipped behind his defender and caught a feed about six yards from the goal from his teammate, Pete Taylor, the Navy captain. Lewis released the shot left handed from among three Army defenders and was immediately drilled to the turf by the Army defenseman stationed behind his right shoulder. Lewis did not see the ball go in the goal but heard the referee's whistle indicating the score. He sprang back to his feet, stared down the Army defender, almost inviting him to do it again next time, and then broke off the gaze, motioning his stick toward the scoreboard, as if to say, You got the hit—but we got the goal.

It didn't take Robbie long to become engrossed in the game. He had never conceived of the game being played with wooden sticks. He marveled at the precision of the stickwork. He couldn't help but notice the extremely physical play.

A few minutes later, Lewis chased down a loose ball on the sideline in front of the Army bench. Somehow he came out with the ball from between two Army players, eluded another, and fired a thirty-yard pass to his streaking attack- and classmate Owen McFadden for a 6-3 lead.

Shortly after Army scored to make it a 6-4 game, Lewis drew his defender to the corner of the field, then raced past him, attacked the goal, gave Army's goalie a dip of the shoulder to draw him down, rose back erect, and neatly rifled the ball over the goalie's right shoulder. 7-4. Again, he was knocked to the turf but chose not to acknowledge that affront.

Then, with seven minutes remaining in the game, Lewis danced past three Army defenders before feeding teammate Tom Morris for a lay-up to make the score 8-4, effectively ending the game. Lewis tallied three goals and two assists in the game and he ended the season with 27 goals and 19 assists.

As the game ended, the players lined up to shake hands. The looks of dejection on the faces of the Army players struck Robbie. Many were wiping tears from their eyes. They had simultaneously suffered two unimaginable fates, a loss to Navy and the loss of their chance at a National Championship. Robbie noted the unspeakable joy of the Navy players and he saw the fine line, a single game, separating total euphoria and total dejection.

"I hope that you've learned something about Captain Lewis, Robbie."

Robbie nodded yes.

"Well, I guess I'd better be going now. I'll see you soon," Red Hawk closed with a smile.

When Robbie woke, he shared the vision with his parents. They were stunned to hear his account of Lewis's career and of the Hall-of-Fame ceremony. John and Mary Jones stared at each other, indicating that they knew there was no way Robbie could have made up—or even dreamed—those facts.

In a much more tolerant tone than the discussion of the first visit, the father proposed, "Robbie, I have an idea. Why don't you start keeping a journal of what you've seen with this Indian boy? We can ask Captain Lewis about it. Deal?"

"Deal."

# N-Star

*The absolute tests are those we face alone.*
—Gerald Coffee
*Beyond Survival*

The limousine was waiting dutifully when Lewis arrived at the airport, and he quickly jumped in, handing the driver the address. He arrived promptly at 7:00, and the Joneses welcomed him inside.

"Thank you so much for coming, Captain Lewis." Lewis immediately knew that they had spoken to Ed Charles. That's good, he thought.

"Thank you for having me. I'm glad to be here."

The hosts went through the necessary formalities, offering drinks and appetizers and making some small talk about the flight and the weather. Over dinner they informed Lewis that they had spoken to Admiral Charles and that he had filled in some of Lewis's background for them. Knowing that Charles must have at least covered the basics, and probably exaggerated some of it, Lewis tried to downplay his past by quipping, "I suppose the fact that you allowed me in means that he didn't tell you everything about me."

During dinner Lewis politely responded to questions concerning his playing days, providing minimal information and whenever possible deflecting credit to his former team-mates. The boy was fascinated. After dinner, the parents politely asked Robbie and his sister to excuse themselves for a little while. The children dutifully left, and Lewis and the parents adjourned to the family's den, bringing their coffee with them.

The family was much more at ease now but still extremely curious about the stick and the books. Lewis allowed the parents to initiate the discussion.

"Again, Captain Lewis..." began Mrs. Jones.

"Jim, please," Lewis interrupted.

"Jim, then. We can't thank you enough for coming. Please forgive our concern, but you have to agree that this whole situation with you and Robbie is quite remarkable. Robbie told us yesterday of a visit he had in which he was taken to your Hall-of-Fame ceremony at the Naval Academy." Lewis smiled and nodded as she continued.

"Of course, as parents our primary concern is that no harm will come to our son. And from the way he has been talking about this stick, it almost seems that it has magical powers, like some sort of witchcraft. We never would have believed this possible, but he is completely convinced that the stick is responsible for these dreams he seems to be having—and he doesn't even call them dreams. He calls them 'visits' because he claims to be totally awake. We just don't want him getting all tied up in an occult phenomenon that he can't get out of. Do you understand?"

"Of course."

"So you believe that these visions or visits are really happening because of the stick?"

"Well, yes, the visions that you described to me on the phone did not surprise me." The parents felt a chill go through their bodies again. "I had many, perhaps hundreds, of visions—visits—myself when I had that stick."

"How is that possible?" Mary pleaded, not wanting to believe that such visions or magical powers were possible.

"Well, you may or may not know that Native Americans

believe that the spirits of the dead come back in tangible form. Once you get past traditional thinking on the afterlife, it becomes easier to accept."

"You'll have to forgive us for struggling with this," said the mother.

"At first it was difficult for me to believe and understand also," Lewis conceded. "My parents never knew the full story of this stick. They mostly left me to my own devices, and I worked hard and kept my nose clean, so they left me alone for the most part. 'Witchcraft,' the word you used before, never came into our vocabulary. I was a relatively happy and healthy kid, so my parents never had real cause for worry. I just enjoyed having the stick and the things I learned through it. There is really only one other person who knows of my true relationship with the stick, and it's no one from my family," Lewis concluded cryptically.

"Is it possible to describe the effect the stick has had on your life?" asked Mary.

"Well, this stick has been a very special part of my life. It's helped me achieve a oneness with the game, with my family, with my job, and that oneness has helped carry me through many challenges in my life. It represents so much to me. I have tried to render honor to the stick, its previous custodians, and the game in the way that I played, and to a greater extent, the way that I have lived my life.

"I was able to maintain a correspondence with Mr. Turnbull for many years after he presented me the stick. I can't tell you how much that meant to me for all those years. I would like to be available to your son for such a correspondence should he desire one. Mr. Turnbull was about fifty-five at the time I met him, and he passed away several years ago at the age of eighty-eight," Lewis closed with a reverent smile.

"Do you know the other men who have been custodians of the stick?" the mother asked.

"It took me some time to fully understand the history of this stick. I don't think I would be able to do justice to its history in a few minutes. What I would like to say, though, is that I'm sure Robbie will gain a great deal of insight into what this stick means—the positive energy, passion, love, respect, and spirit that have been a part of it for all these years."

"Would you mind if Robbie asked you some questions. We know he really wants to."

"Not at all. He's what the stick is all about now."

Robbie and Catherine came into the den. Robbie dove right into the questions.

"Did you do any of these carvings?" Robbie asked.

"Yes, I did do one of the carvings. Can you guess which one?"

"Was it the top one—the big 'N' with the stars?"

Lewis nodded with a smile.

"My dad and I thought that it was some sort of compass pointing to the North Star. Or does it have something to do with Navy?"

"First of all, you should probably know that Native Americans often made carvings or inscriptions on their sticks. The figures, of course, had some sort of personal or spiritual meaning to the player. They also attached various things to their sticks—feathers, claws, teeth and the like. The carving that I did has very special meaning to me.

"Back when I was playing lacrosse and soccer at the Naval Academy, we used to earn varsity letters like most athletes on college and high school teams. But at Navy we also earned what we call an 'N-Star' for our sweaters when we beat Army. It was a big deal back then, and it's still a big deal today. I was fortunate to have earned five such stars.

"I can't imagine a more spirited rivalry in any sport in any school than any Army-Navy game. I think it comes from a shared bond. The academies are similar in their fundamental challenges and goals, as well as all of us being on the same 'team' in defense of our country. We depend upon each other—the Army, Navy, Marines, Air Force, and Coast Guard—when we go into battle. John Feinstein has recently written an excellent book on the history of the Army-Navy football game. It's called *A Civil War*, and most of what you learn about the football rivalry applies to nearly the same degree to every other sport at the academies. I just happen to have a copy of that book for you and your parents."

Lewis pulled the books out of his travel briefcase and handed one each to Robbie and his parents. He also presented Robbie's sister a copy of *The Diary of Anne Frank*.

"It's a great book," Lewis pronounced in regard to the Army-Navy book. "You should read it when you get a chance."

The parents and the boy were enthralled. They recalled their discussion with Admiral Charles and were awed by the notion that they were listening to one of the great players of all time talking about his playing days and career afterwards. This was for real. They didn't want to believe it, but it was.

"Anyway, the 'N-Star' carving is not for my playing days but is in honor of one of my teammates who lettered three times each in lacrosse and soccer. His name was Bill Kearns, and he also earned five stars. He exemplified everything that you would want to see in an athlete and in a person. He was a great naval officer who died in captivity in Vietnam after his plane was shot down. His fellow POW's later told of his extraordinarily noble conduct while in captivity. He was the captain of our team, the consummate team player. He always put other people ahead of himself on the field and in the hall—the dorm. It was no surprise for any of us to hear that when he could ease the suffering of his fellow prisoners-of-war, he would. He did it in a variety of ways, by mending their wounds, and giving them some of the meager food and water rations he received. In fact, he smuggled his own food to fellow prisoners who were weaker than he was. Late at night, when the guards were sleeping, he found a way to crawl through the ceiling of his cell to cells of his comrades, then return unnoticed. He was one of the most heroic people this country has ever known. His comrades say he died of a severe case of malaria he was too weak to fight off, like a great many other POW's who suffered a similar fate.

"He left behind a wife and two small children, a boy and a girl. At the time he was captured they were about four and two. Many of our teammates have set up and contributed to a trust fund for their education. He was the greatest person I ever knew. I carved the 'N-stars' after I learned of his passing to keep his spirit alive in this stick and in the game. I don't know if you recognize the outline of the maps on either side of the 'N,' but on the left side here," he pointed out to Robbie, "is Vietnam. On the right side is Long Island, where Bill and I are from. He was from Kings Park, and I'm from Uniondale. He loved the game as much as anyone I've ever known. His life has truly inspired me in all that I've done since we lost him. You'll see a lot more about what the 'N-Star' means in the Feinstein book."

As Lewis concluded his story, Robbie felt his whole body tingle again.

It was getting late, and Lewis wanted to let the boy enjoy some of the same excitement he had experienced in discovering more about the stick *through* the stick itself rather than through him. The boy would learn plenty in due time, he reminded himself. Lewis made overtures that he didn't want to keep the children up too late. Mr. and Mrs. Jones quickly picked up on the cue and told the children to prepare for bed because Captain Lewis had to fly back to California early in the morning.

Lewis thanked the family for their hospitality and extended the same offer he had at their first meeting, "I won't impose anything on you all, but I will answer questions as best I can. If you don't mind, perhaps I can take the liberty of sending Robbie a book on his birthday." Then looking at the sister's wide eyes, "And his sister, as well, as Mr. Turnbull did for me. I'm scheduled to be in town again in about three weeks. I'm in this part of the country about once a month for two or three days on business—perhaps we could meet again?"

The Joneses nodded their assent. As Lewis strode slowly down the walkway toward the waiting limousine, he soaked in the warm breeze and smiled at the waning full moon.

# Long Island, New York

After another interval of a month, Robbie began to wonder when Red Hawk might return. That night Red Hawk came to Robbie, who was very happy to see his new friend.

*"Hi, Robbie."*

*"Hi!"*

*"How about tonight you tell me where you'd like to go?"*

*"Really? Anywhere?"*

*"Sure. What do you think?"*

*"Well, I guess it would be neat to see how Captain Lewis received the stick. Can we do that?"*

*"O.K. Let's go to a town called Uniondale, New York—on Long Island. It's March of 1959."*

*After a long day of meetings with executives of the Long Island Rail Road, Doug Turnbull drove past a small high school on his way to dinner. As he drove, he saw a boy in the dark under a single light, practicing his lacrosse skills on a handball court. After finishing dinner, Turnbull drove back past the boy who was still working his skills.*

*The next night, Turnbull drove past again. This time the boy was practicing under the same light in a steady drizzle. Again*

*Turnbull saw him on his return trip.*

*On the third night, Turnbull's meetings had run much later than the previous days', and he did not expect to see the boy out so late. Yet there he was, pounding away on the wall. Very impressive, the man thought. He decided to stop and watch the boy. The youngster did not notice that Turnbull had parked nearby and begun to walk slowly toward him. As he watched, Turnbull appropriately kept a respectful distance from the boy. He was most intrigued to see the boy 'shadow boxing' an imaginary defender as he practiced his footwork, dodging, and stick position. Though the man had grown up, played, and presently lived in an area famous for its brilliant high school and collegiate lacrosse, Turnbull had never seen these training tactics employed by a youngster.*

*The boy executed the moves over and over, dodging and shooting. After all six of his balls had slipped away from him, the boy took a break to recover them. Turnbull took the opportunity to approach the boy.*

*"I've seen you here three nights in a row. Do you come here every night?" Turnbull opened.*

*"Yes, sir, just about every night if it's not raining," the young Lewis replied.*

*"It was raining last night."*

*"Not that hard, sir."*

*"Please allow me to introduce myself. I am Doug Turnbull."*

*"My pleasure, sir. I'm Jimmy Lewis."*

*"Do you go to school here?"*

*"Yes, sir, right there," Lewis pointed, "Uniondale High School."*

*"What grade are you in?"*

*"Ninth."*

*"Well, Jimmy, I have to say that I'm most impressed with your training regimen. I'm from Baltimore, and we like to think our boys are dedicated to the game. But the work I've seen you do would put them to shame."*

*Lewis did not know how to respond. Turnbull continued. "So, do they give you homework at Uniondale High School?"*

"Yes, sir. I usually go home after practice for dinner, then do my homework for an hour or so, and come back while it's still light. Sometimes I stay after dark."

Lewis had collected all of his balls.

"Don't let me hold you up. Keep throwing, son," Turnbull offered.

Lewis continued with his drills. Turnbull watched him carefully.

"Did you play lacrosse, sir?"

"Yes, but a long time ago. I haven't played in years."

"What team did you play for?"

"Well, in high school I played at Poly in Baltimore, then Johns Hopkins, then the Mount Washington Club."

Lewis felt a new respect for the visitor, knowing that Hopkins and Mount Washington represented the best the game had to offer. He had never seen either team play, but he imagined that his visitor was a famous player.

"Would you happen to have a game tomorrow?"

"Yes, sir, we do. We're playing Massapequa at 4:30 here at home. Right there on that field. They're pretty good."

"Mind if I come and watch?"

"No. That would be great."

Lewis went home very excited to have met Turnbull, and told he his mother that the Hopkins player would come watch him play.

Red Hawk then took Robbie to the game the next day. They saw Turnbull arrive just as the game began.

Turnbull watched Lewis carefully. He knew the boy had something special and could very well be the one he wanted to pass the stick to. Turnbull's presence inspired Lewis to play harder than ever. He scored two goals and had two assists in a winning effort. Turnbull congratulated the boy after the game. "Good job, Jimmy. You did an excellent job. And your team played well."

"Thank you, sir. But I could have done a lot better. I need to figure out why I lose the ball and why it takes so long to pass or shoot it out of the stick. I practice so much, but the stick and I don't seem to work at times. I don't enjoy making mistakes—that's why you saw me at the wall. I know I can figure this game out."

Turnbull was impressed. He had intentionally not made mention of that part of the boy's performance, though he had noted it.

"I think that comes as a natural consequence of your aggressiveness, Jimmy. I really liked how hard you tried to make things happen."

"Thanks, but I'm still not happy. I've tried to work on it, but I'm not really getting any better. I'm working on different ways to carry my stick with one hand so that I won't lose the ball and also get rid of it quickly, but I just can't get it to work."

Turnbull had noticed the unique style and was glad to hear that the boy was consciously attempting it. At that instant, Turnbull realized that this was, in fact, the boy who needed to have the stick. He had clung particularly close to the stick for several years but knew that eventually he'd have to pass it along. It was time. The stick was not a possession, not someone's property to be passed within one family. It was a tool, and when in the hands of the right person, it would change their life. The stick was not about the past, grieving, or despair. It was about the future, life, and hope. He had only recently allowed himself to seek the next recipient.

Turnbull's searches of the playgrounds, sandlots, and fields of Baltimore had not produced the results he had hoped for. He had finally found the right person. Jimmy Lewis had the energy, talent, imagination, and work ethic. This boy is going to make a difference—Turnbull knew it. He smiled within. It felt completely right for the first time. He mocked himself in a whisper, "A Long Islander! I should have known it would happen like this."

Just then Lewis's mother approached the boy and gave him a hug, which he only grudgingly acknowledged, shaking loose as quickly as possible before his teammates might see it.

"Mom, this is Mr. Turnbull. He's the man I met last night. The one from Johns Hopkins."

"Doug Turnbull, ma'am," Turnbull offered as he extended his

hand. *"Your son is a rather remarkable player."*

*"Thank you. He loves to play, and so does his brother Johnny. He's on the varsity. I like lacrosse a lot as well, but it's not always easy for a mother to watch."*

*"I understand. My mother suffered through many, many games my brother and I played."* Turnbull offered with a smile in admiration of his recently-deceased mother.

*"What brings you to town, Mr. Turnbull?"*

*"I work for the railroad in Baltimore. I'm here for some meetings with the people of your Long Island Rail Road. I head back tomorrow. With your permission, I'd be honored if I could meet Jimmy at his training spot—the handball wall—for a few pointers that have been passed on to me."*

*"That would be great, sure. Thank you."*

*"O.K., Jimmy, I'll see you tomorrow then."*

*"I'll be waiting for you, sir."*

After his morning meeting, Turnbull met young Lewis at the handball court to study his mechanics and to provide some refinements to his training program. When Turnbull arrived, Jimmy was already well along with his regimen. Turnbull marveled at the boy's ability and focus.

*"So you said that you were trying to work on your vertical stick position?"*

*"Yes, sir. I've tried to get it to the point where I could use it in a game but it won't work."*

Turnbull smiled. *"Jimmy, I hope you realize that you are going against the grain. I mean, what you are trying is very different from how we all grew up with the game, and I don't think anyone has approached playing quite like this. Certainly no one in Baltimore has ever seen anything like this before."*

*"I really wouldn't know, sir. It just seems like the best way to carry and protect my stick and get rid of the ball. I mean, if I can keep the stick away from the defense, they won't really be able to check it."*

Turnbull watched as the boy attempted to hold his stick upright, cradle, then shoot. The boy's movements were remarkably good, but still not effective.

"Here, let me try for a second," Turnbull asked, accepting Jimmy's stick. "You know, Jimmy, back in the 1930's and '40's my brother Jack was a fantastic attackman. He was the only one I've ever seen who came close to being able to control his stick like you are attempting. He came upon the thought fairly late in his career and was only beginning to perfect it himself. He died in World War II, so I never got to see him master it. He totally dominated the game when he played—one newspaper-man even called him the 'Babe Ruth of Lacrosse'—but he never did completely develop his concepts as he hoped he would."

Turnbull continued, "How long have you been working on this?"

"I don't know. A few months, I guess. My sticks have been difficult to handle. My brother and I even made home-made sticks with a broom handle, string, cloth, and metal wire—just to see if I could get a better feel and balance. Those didn't really work, but they helped me see where the problems are. So I've tried to modify my sticks. I have been able to get it close but still haven't been able to get it right. It's been frustrating."

Turnbull was amazed by what he was hearing. How could a boy of this age have considered all of these subtle but significant aspects of lacrosse?

"Jimmy, it seems like some patience would be good here. You've certainly taken a good look at this. I have something that might help."

With that, Turnbull produced the leather bag which Robbie recognized immediately—his bag, with the same contents! Robbie and Red Hawk continued to watch.

"Here, try this one," Turnbull offered as he slid the stick out of its bag.

Lewis held the stick in disbelief. He instantly sensed his intimate connection with the stick. He slowly cradled a ball, switched *hands back and forth and knew that with this he was about to achieve his goal and vision of how he should play the game. He threw the ball at a mark on the wall, striking it several times in a row. Turnbull detected the boy's new-found inspiration and felt Jack's presence among them.*

*"I've never hit the same spot like that—all in a row, Mr. Turnbull," Lewis said excitedly. The boy hit it several more times, and then looked at Turnbull.*

*"Did you know I would be able to do that with this stick?"*

*"Well, I had a feeling. Would you like to keep it?"*

*Lewis was too stunned to accept. "I can't, sir. I mean, why me?"*

*"Please accept it—you'll learn why later on. Try cradling behind your shoulder."*

*Lewis tried it for the first time and he felt a perfect balance and fit. He'd been waiting and experimenting for months to attain this feel. He gently rocked the stick back-and-forth. He switched to his left hand with the same perfection. He knew where the ball was without having to make any unnecessary movements or looks at the stick. This was special.*

*Lewis suddenly froze as a vision entered his mind's eye. The dazed boy reported it to Turnbull. "Wow! I just saw a vision of an old-time player dodging a defenseman with his stick tucked behind his shoulder."*

*"Jim, there is a pretty good chance that player was Jack. I told you he had pulled off that move a couple times."*

*"It looked so natural. Why haven't players been able to do it before," Lewis asked, as if he had become a master in just a few minutes.*

*"I have to believe it's been a function of the weight and asymmetry of the stick, Jimmy. Players just haven't been able to control the stick in that position—until now."*

*The self-confidence that overtook Lewis was intense and immediate. He suddenly felt that he had the instrument that would allow him to reach his potential. He thought that he was no longer* bridled by the limitations of every stick he'd used in the past. He was a very good athlete, strong, incredibly quick on his feet and with his hands. All these attributes had been hampered on the lacrosse field whenever he picked up the ball. This would no longer be the case. He hoped to have an opportunity to use the stick in the next game. Lewis and Turnbull spent the next two hours tinkering with the stick. Lewis tried to improve his release and found this stick the smoothest he had ever touched. He switched hands from right to left and left to right from the vertical position. Balance, efficiency, quick release, the boy thought. This is so smooth. I can do this!

Finally, Turnbull presented the wooden box to Lewis. "Jimmy, these gifts have been passed to me—and now I pass them to you. I believe they'll provide you with insight and wisdom far beyond anything you've ever conceived. Please enjoy them while you have them and then pass them along to another at a time of your choosing. And please render the appropriate respect to these gifts and the game of lacrosse."

Lewis began his walk home, whispering a bit deviously to himself, "I don't think I'll tell Johnny about this just yet. A little more for the sibling rivalry wouldn't be anything new."

Robbie awoke from his sleep with nearly the same sense of destiny as Lewis had acquired in the dream. "This stick is really, really special," he jotted quickly in his journal before he headed to breakfast.

# The Wall

*Good stickwork is acquired only by hard, earnest,*
*and sometimes monotonous practice.*
—W. Kelso Morrill
*Lacrosse*

As he'd planned, Lewis visited the family about three weeks after the last meeting. He asked Robbie where the nearest wall might be for them to practice their skills. Robbie informed him that there was a suitable wall about four blocks away at an elementary school. They made the short walk and began throwing on the wall.

"Would you mind if I give you a couple of pointers, Robbie?"

"That would be great."

"I've spent thousands of hours on the wall, Robbie. Mr. Turnbull showed me some drills I could practice. He and his brother Jack used to do these on the side of a barn. Maybe I can show you some of the things he taught me. I think they're still useful today.

"Mr. Turnbull used to tell me that having a system was the key to success. And so he showed me these drills in sets. Sets of tens, twenties, and hundreds, until I started doing them by time. I knew that it would take five or ten minutes to do a certain number. So I'd recommend that you develop a plan and be systematic and disciplined about your approach to this part of your game. Block off a certain time of day or days during the week to do this.

"Mr. Turnbull also used to tell me that in the course of a year with just one hour a week we would get as much work as we would in about eight seasons of regular practices. Looking back at his assessment, I completely agree. You simply can't get to a high level in this game or any other for that matter, without putting in the time. Mr. Turnbull sometimes called this 'the work in a vacuum' with no other players, coaches, or parents—just you, a ball, and the wall. You work and hone your skills here and then get to perfect them in practice and against excellent competition in games. But this is also where you can spend the time to think of new ways— better ways—to play and succeed in the game. It may be a subtle change or an increase in how quickly and accurately you perform the fundamentals. But, in the aggregate, your total grasp of the skills, your performance and your confidence will improve. He also used to talk to me about the obligation a player has to his team to work at improvement. He'd say that a team could not reach its full potential unless all players did. I still think he's right."

Lewis went through the array of skills, stopping at each part to observe Robbie's mechanics and to offer small but meaningful corrections.

They started by throwing straight over the top, then around the clock at two-hour intervals on both hands. Lewis talked as he demonstrated and encouraged Robbie to keep throwing as he offered suggestions. Lewis then backed Robbie away from the wall to about twenty-five yards to work on shooting the ball.

"On this, Robbie, work on macroscopic motion, your arms, shoulders, trunk, and legs. Get your hands up and out. Work on your three-quarter shot. After you get the mechanics, work on refining the shot. Aim for targets. You will ultimately want to shoot on the run. You can do that on the wall, too. This drill is also good for catching hard passes. You can work your shooting around the clock as well." Lewis demonstrated the skills a few times and then critiqued Robbie again.

Lewis rolled the ball into the wall underhand so that it would return along the ground. "This is a great way to work on your ground ball skills, Robbie. Get your body low as it returns, scoop the ball, and then get your stick up by your helmet as quickly as possible. You should include a few sets of these every time."

Then Lewis showed Robbie how to work on catching bad passes, a critical skill. "Here, throw to the wrong side of your helmet. You should move a little closer to the wall, maybe six to eight yards. Catch the ball backhanded, and draw it back across your face. You can also throw balls low or wide. When you catch a bad pass, get your stick vertical and to your helmet as quickly as possible, just like on ground balls."

Robbie listened and worked to absorb all he could. Lewis then showed Robbie a series of alternating-hand exercises, changing hands right to left and left to right unconsciously as he talked. The boy marveled at the speed of the changes and the precision of the man's throws, exactly where he intended and with a nice zip on each.

"Oh, yeah, have some fun, too. After you've completed some strong sets, reward yourself with some fun stuff, behind the back, one hand, between the legs. You know, break up the monotony a little. I used to end my sets by trying to hit the same spot on the wall, say fifty times. I know there is one mark on my wall back home that I hit at least 10,000 times—with each hand. We'll look at some other skills next time we get a chance, some dodging, maybe. There is much more you can do. Most of it is just a function of your imagination and desire to improve yourself and your team.

"And one last thing...work on deception. Make some fundamentals look similar up to the last moment of execution and then, as a hunter lures his prey, strike with a different movement—as if you have sprung a trap or pulled away the bait as the hunter strikes. This is how you can improve your dodging and scoring."

Robbie couldn't believe the depth of insight that Lewis possessed and the value of his assistance. He could feel his improvement immediately.

# A True Hero

*These laid the world away; poured out the red*
*Sweet wine of youth; gave up the years to be*
*Of work and joy, and that unhoped serene,*
*That men call age; and those who would have been,*
*Their sons, they gave, their immortality.*
—Rupert Brooke
*The War Sonnets*

Red Hawk appeared to Robbie on the next full moon.

*"Would you like to go anywhere in particular, Robbie?"*

*"Since I heard Mr. Turnbull say that Jack had died in World War II, I started to wonder what happened."*

*"Well, let's go take a look."*

*Red Hawk took Robbie to Station 143, North Pickenham, England on October 18, 1944 to the 44th Bomb Group Ready Room.*

*"Attention on deck!" called First Lieutenant Michael Taylor, as Lieutenant Colonel Jack Turnbull entered the ready room.*

*Turnbull began his briefing quickly, "Seats, gentlemen. This morning our mission is to Leverkusen, Germany, approximately 10 miles northeast of Cologne, to attack a chemical works located there. We will have a total of 31 B-24's in our group. We will conduct this mission exactly as we have for the last ten sorties. Our fighter support will lead us in at exactly 1450. That will provide us ten minutes over the target, just enough time to drop our payloads before we expect to encounter resistance. However, be prepared for* opposition during the entire sortie. I say again, be prepared for opposition. I'll fly with Lieutenant Taylor in the lead aircraft of the 67th Squadron. Major McLaughlin, a weather update..."

"Yes, sir. The weather is expected to be clear over the target area. Clouds will be building from the west during our mission, and we may encounter them on the return flight."

"Very well," Turnbull took charge again, "Any questions?

"Very well. Chaplain."

Robbie looked on as the chaplain led the group in prayer.

"Lord, give our men the strength, courage, confidence, and skill to execute this mission and return safely. In your name, we pray...Amen."

"Amen," was offered clearly but quietly by all the airmen.

Lieutenant Taylor caught up to Turnbull on the way out of the ready room. "Colonel, will you be flying in the co-pilot's seat? I'll make the arrangements."

"No, lieutenant, I generally don't take that seat. I feel it's more important for you, as the commander of the aircraft, to remain in the Command Pilot seat. I won't disrupt the integrity of your crew and their training. Is that satisfactory?"

"Yes, sir, just wanted to check first. Some Command Pilots insist on taking that seat."

"I understand. I don't. I'll sit behind your co-pilot."

"Yes, sir, Colonel. My crew will be ready in five minutes."

Red Hawk then took Robbie into the aircraft during its flight. Robbie immediately noticed the noisy, cold, and cramped quarters. He watched in awe as the men conducted their flight.

Just a few miles from their target, Technical Sergeant Jerome Anderson startled Robbie, calling across the plane's intercom, "Fire! We have a fire in the bomb bay!"

Robbie felt his heart go directly into his throat and looked at Red Hawk.

"Do you want to leave, Robbie?"

"I'm O.K."

*The bombardier, 1st Lieutenant Randall Rollins, requested and received permission to jettison his payload, taking the fire with it.*

*"Doors open! Bombs away! Fire is out! Door closed and locked!" Rollins reported to Taylor.*

*"Roger. Any idea how it started?"*

*"Not yet," Rollins reported as he strained his eyes through the heavy cloud cover to see where the bombs may have landed and with what effect. "We'll take a look."*

*Jack Turnbull sat stoically behind the co-pilot as the crew handled the emergency. By the book, Jack thought to himself. Good job. Continue on. Stay focused, lieutenant. Stay focused.*

*Taylor continued to lead the formation to the target area. All planes dropped their bomb load as scheduled, and the formation met no resistance. Well, a successful mission so far, Jack thought, despite the fire onboard his adopted plane. Don't know about losses—no bombing results—tough clouds. Wish I could get some idea. Well, it's not the first time we couldn't tell how we did. Continue on. Stay focused.*

*Just a few minutes later, Jack saw the storm clouds building quickly before his formation. Just after he noticed it, Taylor reported it to him.*

*"Colonel, looks like some bad weather ahead. At least 3-4,000 feet above us and it doesn't look like we can get around it, either."*

*Jack glanced quickly at the plane's altimeter, which read 24,000 feet. He knew instantly that there would be no going over the storm. "Clouds will be building—my butt!" he thought. The plane simply could not get that high that fast.*

*"Correct, lieutenant. Looks like we'll just have to split the formation and go through. We've done this many times before. Nice and easy," Jack offered calmly as a confidence-builder for the young New Yorker as they entered the clouds and visibility went to near-zero. Master yourself, Jack thought to himself as he prepared to help guide the young pilot through the challenge.*

*Robbie was frozen in fear as he watched the clouds swallow the aircraft and felt the turbulence shake every bit of the plane.*

*Taylor and his crew calmly handled the turbulence and continued flying by their instruments, knowing that the integrity of the formation depended on his smoothness and abilities. Suddenly the plane banked sharply to the left, perhaps struck by another bomber. The pilot struggled to regain stability of the craft. At this point, Jack instructed, "Be strong, lieutenant. Center the needle. Center the needle!"*

*Red Hawk took Robbie from the plane at that point seconds before the plane plummeted to the ground and ended the lives of too many heroes.*

*"Are you doing O.K., Robbie?" Red Hawk asked as he saw how shaken the boy was.*

*"What happened to the plane!?"*

*"This is going to be hard to watch...."*

*"I can handle it. I need to know."*

*"Are you sure?"*

*"I'm sure."*

*"O.K., let's go to Baltimore."*

*Robbie and Red Hawk next appeared at the home of Jack's mother, "Mum" Turnbull, 2111 Sulgrave Avenue, Baltimore, Maryland on Election Day, November 7, 1944.*

*Mum Turnbull had risen from her breakfast table at 9 a.m. and changed into a dress in order to perform her citizen's duty to vote in the general election. She proudly clipped on her set of pilot's wings, a gift from Jack upon his earning his qualification. While it was a task she performed every day—on every sweater, blouse, dress, jacket (and she would eventually be buried with)—today she did so with a great deal of melancholy. She had been notified that Jack had been reported missing two weeks earlier and hadn't received any more recent news. No news, in this case, she thought, was bad news. With each passing day she had a greater feeling of foreboding.*

*She walked to the front closet to get her coat when the doorbell startled her. She looked at her sister May, her housemate since her husband's passing. She briefly hoped the visitor might be a neighbor coming to walk her to the polling station. That hope lasted but a second, when a chill ran through her body. She knew before she opened the door. She looked at May and said, "This is it."*

*She took a deep breath and opened the door slowly. Her breath left her lungs, and she briefly felt faint. Before her stood an army officer and a chaplain, certain to bear the news she feared most.*

*"Mrs. Turnbull?" the officer asked delicately. Mum offered an acknowledgment with a barely perceptible nod.*

*"Mrs. Turnbull, I am Colonel Finney. This is Reverend Sheedy. May we come in?"*

*Still not speaking, Mum opened the door further, allowing the men to enter. She walked to her kitchen table and gestured for the men to sit. They waited for her and May to do so first.*

*Finney began, "Mrs. Turnbull, it is with great regret that I must inform you that your son, Lieutenant Colonel John I. 'Jack' Turnbull has been killed in action over a small town called Petegem-aan-de-Leie/Deinze, Belgium, about nine miles southwest of Ghent and near the German border."*

*Mum did not move or respond. Her face betrayed the slightest hint that she wanted to know how and why, so the chaplain continued softly, "Mrs. Turnbull, your son was assigned as Command Pilot for a mission over Leverkusen, Germany. His group made a successful run over the site, but encountered a severe thunderstorm on their return to base. It appears that the aircraft that Jack was in was struck by another in its group, causing both to crash."*

*Mum's eyes asked for just a little more information.*

*Sheedy continued, "Nuns from nearby Convent Gesticht van Den H. Joseph responded to the accident, treating two conscious survivors, Staff Sergeants George Sims and Lawrence Lindsay, who had miraculously been able to parachute out of Jack's plane. All the others on board the planes, twelve in all, were killed in the crash except for Jack. The nuns found him breathing but unconscious. They were able to transport Jack to their convent and treat him while they awaited proper medical assistance. Unfortunately,*

*Lieutenant Colonel Turnbull died within 48 hours, having regaining only brief periods of consciousness. Our nation mourns his death as he was a fine officer and a loving son. "*

*Mum continued to sit silently, this time her eyes dropping and blinking back her tears.*

*The colonel, attending now to the unpleasant business concerning the disposition of the body, continued, "Mrs. Turnbull, your son's body has been interred at Henri Chappelle Cemetery, Belgium. He and his comrades were briefly buried in the World War I American Cemetery at Flanders Field, until we could arrange for a proper military burial at Chappelle Cemetery. Jack was buried with full military honors."*

*The colonel slid a folder to the middle of the table with all of the pertinent information on the specifics of Jack's burial. He continued, "Mrs. Turnbull, the United States of America can never know your grief and can never compensate you for this loss. Perhaps it would be of some comfort for you to know that I trained with Jack here in the Maryland Air Corps, and I have never known a finer pilot or a finer person. I share your tremendous loss."*

*Mum continued to sit in silence for several more minutes, still blinking back tears. "Thank you," she finally whispered.*

*"Is there anything that we may do for you, Mrs. Turnbull?" offered the chaplain.*

*"No. No, thank you," Mum whispered again as she stood and escorted the men to her door. As she opened the door, she turned to her sister.*

*"Are you ready, May?" Mum asked in regard to their original plan to cast their votes, "Let's go."*

*Robbie was terribly shaken by those two scenes but persisted in his questions to Red Hawk.*

*"Mr. Lewis said that the Turnbull Award was named in honor of Jack Turnbull. Can you tell me about that?"*

*"Well, I can show you some of that if you would like to see it. Its not nearly as hard to watch as what you just saw."*

*"Sure," Robbie said, trying to be enthusiastic, but he had clearly*

*lost some of his optimism in the last few minutes.*

*Red Hawk took Robbie to Homewood Field, Johns Hopkins University, Baltimore, Maryland on June 7, 1946.*

*Midshipman Second Class Stewart McLean stood along the sideline of the fabled field, next to his attack mate from the U.S. Naval Academy, freshman phenom J.H.L. "Lee" Chambers. Four other midshipman stood next to Chambers and their coach, William H. "Dinty" Moore, who stood like a proud father next to them all. It was half-time of the 1946 North-South College All-Star game, the annual showcase of the best collegiate lacrosse talent in the country. On this special night Moore had been selected to be the south team's coach. Both teams were lined up on their respective sidelines for a solemn ceremony. A crowd of some 3,500 spectators stood silent as Mum Turnbull was escorted to the center of the field by her eldest son, Doug. The crowd and the All-Stars were well aware of the significance of Mrs. Turnbull's presence. They knew that this was to be a tribute to Jack.*

*The public address announcer began, "Ladies and gentlemen, today we are honored to have Mrs. Elizabeth 'Mum' Turnbull, escorted by her son, Doug, Hopkins's great four-time first-team All-America, here to present a special award in honor of her son Jack, who perished in service to his country almost two years ago. The Mount Washington Lacrosse Club, Jack's former club team and, as you well know, the preeminent team in the country, has endeavored to award a trophy in Jack's honor and memory to the outstanding attackman in the country who 'best emulated the example of Jack Turnbull in good sportsmanship, fair play, field leadership, ability to both feed and score, and who is able to aide the defense.'"*

*The midshipmen stood at attention as Mrs. Turnbull arrived at midfield. McLean thought of his plebe teammate, Lee Chambers, and what a phenomenal player he had been all season, the uncharacteristic poise, and the thirty-five goals, for a freshman. McLean glanced over toward the North sideline and saw Alfred "Shorty" Haussmann, the senior first-team All-America In-home from Army.*

Surely one of those two players will be honored. McLean then thought of Jack Turnbull, whom his father had known through the Maryland Army Air Corps. He remembered seeing Jack play when he was a boy. What a great tragedy, what a terrible loss.

The public address announcer continued, "Mrs. Turnbull would like to present the handsome cup which Doug is holding to the inaugural recipient of the Lieutenant Colonel John Iglehart Turnbull Memorial Award..."

McLean stood poised to applaud Chambers or Haussmann.

"Midshipman Second Class Stewart McLean, United States Naval Academy."

Dazed by the announcement, McLean looked to his left at Chambers who offered him a smile and a nod to proceed to the center of the field. McLean slowly left his post on the sideline and began to make his way to midfield to greet Mrs. Turnbull. He stood at attention in front of her, his chin and lips quivering, vainly attempting to hold back his tears. Mrs. Turnbull greeted him with her characteristic warm smile, extending her hand. McLean noticed the pilot's wings clipped onto the lapel of Mrs. Turnbull's dress and immediately understood their meaning. He grasped her hand in return.

"Congratulations, Stewart, you have been a credit to this great game. Thank you for being the first player to honor Jack. We could not have wished for a more appropriate choice," she said with impeccable grace and dignity.

While valiantly attempting to maintain his military bearing McLean surrendered to his tears. Doug Turnbull shook his hand and presented him the beautiful cup, with his named engraved upon it. McLean was oblivious to the cheers of the crowd, who were clearly in agreement with the choice. A military man seemed only appropriate.

Still stunned and overwhelmed, McLean was only able to reply, "This will forever be the greatest moment of my life, ma'am. I will cherish this as long as I live."

McLean returned to the sideline to the hugs and handshakes

of his teammates and coaches. Most notably, Lee Chambers, who would be honored with the same award three years later, hugged him warmly. McLean had eased Chambers's plebe year at the Naval Academy and had graciously deferred, and even catered, to Chambers's immense talent, when less-secure upper-classmen would have attempted to keep the brash, young colt in his place. Dinty Moore then embraced McLean, who said, "Coach, I cannot believe that I deserve this award. They must have made a mistake."

Moore looked straight into McLean's now-swollen eyes, and said, "Don't ever think that you don't deserve this award. Jack Turnbull was a great player and great man, and so are you. You have just placed your own stamp on the history of this game and set the standard for all future recipients. Thanks for letting me be a part of it."

McLean's parents were overcome with joy and humility in the stands. His mother saw his father shed a tear for the first time since she'd met him thirty-seven years before. His father made his way to the chain-link fence behind the players' bench to relieve his son of the Trophy and give him an abbreviated hug. McLean sat down on the bench, slumped over to cover his face with his hands. His teammates, particularly his fellow midshipmen, strolled by one or two at a time to pat his shoulder. For several minutes McLean did not move. Then he suddenly shook off his emotions, put on his helmet, and returned to the sideline.

Robbie continued to watch in amazement as the South team erased a 9-2 deficit at the half and executed a superhuman rally to tie the game at eleven, as Chambers scored with less than a minute left to play. After three extra periods, the teams were knotted at fourteen. Chambers finished the game with a record seven goals.

Robbie stared at Red Hawk in disbelief at all he had seen during the visit.

"That's a little bit about Jack Turnbull, but there's a lot more. He was a truly special person," Red Hawk paused when he saw how worn Robbie had become, "but we'll save that for another time."

Robbie woke from this visit completely exhausted. This

trip had been much more emotional than the others had been. His parents saw the fatigue in his eyes when he conveyed the essence of the dream.

# Respect the Game

Lewis visited Robbie again on the third Sunday of the month, and they walked together to the wall.

"What would you like to talk about today, Robbie?"

"I've been wondering about what you mean by 'Respect the Game.' Can you tell me about that?"

Lewis began his answer as they walked, "Well, that's a rather difficult question. I must say that my philosophy of the game reflects the many great players and coaches with whom I had an opportunity to work during my career. Most notable among those people were Terry McDonald, my high school coach, who had a tremendous impact on me and countless other high school players, and Willis P. 'Bildy' Bilderback, my coach at the Naval Academy, who also taught me a great deal about the game and myself. I was also extremely fortunate to have played with tremendous athletes who were dedicated to improving themselves and their teams. They were always an inspiration to me. And, of course, all of my discussions with Mr. Turnbull and Red Hawk. What I have to say about 'Respect the Game' is really the sum of the interaction with all of those wonderful men. I should also say at this point that most of what I will say probably applies to all of your athletic endeavors, most of your schooling, and regular work. So let me give it a try.

"'Respect the Game' is a concept that takes some time to understand. I think that its full appreciation is gained over a period of time and usually corresponds to the amount of effort and work you've invested in the game. I think at its core, 'Respect the Game' means to play the game as it was meant to be played in antiquity, but within the current rules."

Robbie listened intently as they continued to walk.

"Above all else, the essence of lacrosse was and is its test of endurance and physical strength. So in order to play the game well today, a player must be strong, physical, and in top shape. Only after achieving a sound physical base can a player's physical courage and skill become useful. Lacrosse of today requires fidelity to the age-old and inherent physical rigors of the game. To play lacrosse at its highest level a player must be strong of mind, body, and spirit and must not yield to fatigue."

Lewis lobbed a ball off the wall to Robbie as they arrived, and they both began to work the skills Lewis had demonstrated on his last visit.

"Also, to respect the game, a player needs to develop the skills required by the game, to be able to handle his stick as though it were an extension of his arm. Players today need to be adept at throwing, catching, scooping, dodging, and shooting with either hand. This requires a great deal of concentrated and systematic effort. In order for a team to play at its highest level, each player must contribute his best efforts. This means to exercise the proper skill at the right time, which quite often means using the 'proper' hand. Like this, Robbie.

"Say you're running along the left sideline against pressure and need to make a pass to a teammate thirty yards away and upfield. You *must* throw the ball left handed. If you don't, your mechanics will suffer and you'll either throw a poor pass or be checked. So being able to use both hands is important. Back in the old days, most players were restricted to one hand. Mr. Turnbull pointed this out to me when I first met him. He encouraged me to learn to play with both hands, so I worked hard at it. He talked of balance, of equal skill left or right, as balanced as the stick he gave me. I once spoke to Tom Mitchell, a Turnbull Award recipient from the Naval Academy Class of 1961, who told me that he played every fall season at USNA with his left hand exclusively in order to become more comfortable and adept with that hand. Mike Buzzell, another recipient from Navy, told me the same thing. I think there is a lot to be learned from Tom's and Buzz's approach. Young players today can exercise that tactic in fall ball, summer league, and camp.

"I think that sportsmanship and team spirit also come into respecting the game. This is perhaps more reflective of the game and the role of athletics in society today. One of the roles of lacrosse in Native American life was to prepare young men to become warriors for combat. As a result, games were often extremely rough and physical. Preparing for war was, and still is, serious business. The elders in the tribes who had engaged in battle with other tribes or with European settlers knew the horrors of such engagements. War is not for the faint of heart or body. A tribe's entire safety and way of life were frequently determined by the outcome of a particular battle.

"The ancient Greeks knew this as well. You can see from the modern Olympic events that physical strength, speed, endurance, and close hand-to-hand combat skills were highly prized. Again, all of these physical attributes aided the clan's safety. Warfare has evolved, some might say devolved, quite a bit over the centuries. Today, direct physical 'mano-a-mano' engagements don't play *as* crucial a role in warfare—though physical rigor is still a critical and necessary element of training and on the battlefield. And there's no doubt in my mind that long-term physical, mental, and emotional endurance are critical to success in war. When I was a fighter pilot we all knew that there were no points for second place."

They continued to throw against the wall.

"So sports have evolved from being ancillary training for war to an end in themselves. Our society today continues to place a high value on physical prowess and, I believe, correctly so. It has been the key to the survival of the race. But it seems to me now that knowledge is the real key to power in our world, not necessarily individual physical strength. We now live in a society that generally rewards education more than brawn. Nonetheless, it is not difficult to accept the inherent value of physical strength, speed, and endurance as these can contribute to and be representative of good health.

"Yet despite all of the cruel and barbaric aspects of armed conflict, there has also been a significant human element implicit in war. That remarkable aspect has been reflected in the victor's treatment of the defeated and prisoners captured in battle. In only the most barbaric instances would entire groups of innocent non-combatants—the elderly, women, and children—be slaughtered after the outcome of a battle had been decided. After hostilities have ended prisoners are likewise treated humanely and repatriated to their home-lands. Though there are surely countless historical examples of violations of these general precepts—the treatment of American prisoners of war in Vietnam comes immediately to mind—fair treatment of the captured has long been a part of the human endeavor. And so it is today.

"So as athletics have developed over the centuries from a more direct role in the preparation for combat to what they are today—a means to physical fitness, physical prowess, physical courage, teamwork, and many other laudable traits—sportsmanship has taken on more importance. I think it is important to prepare and play the games as if 'for battle,' but to win and lose graciously because it is, after all, a game and not war. It is also important not to attempt to deliberately injure an opposing player. The game should be played within the established rules as *hard* as it can be played, but at all times fairly. I've seen war, and I've seen peace. Sports are not war—nor should they be. They should be a physical and emotional test, yes, but they are not war."

Facing Lewis Robbie listened intently as he worked his skills.

"Robbie, don't underestimate the significance of the Johns Hopkins University Turnbull-Reynolds Award for Outstanding Sportsmanship and Leadership which is sponsored by the Class of 1932. The men of that class were members of the undefeated Hopkins team that represented the United States in the Los Angeles Olympics and won the Gold Medal. They obviously feel pretty strongly about sportsmanship as it was clearly one of the shining traits of each of those heroic men. You know about Jack Turnbull. Pete Reynolds was an All-America cover point—defenseman—who died on the Bataan Death March, also in World War II.

"Team spirit is another aspect worth mentioning at this point. One of the things that I've found over the years, particularly as a naval officer, is that leadership is extremely difficult—much more difficult than I'd ever have imagined when I was your age. It's far too easy for people to be negative. My high school coach did us a great service by stressing the phrase, 'Don't expect anything to be easy. You're not going to accomplish anything *just because!*' He taught us to stay positive and to support each other, regardless of the situation. He always stressed the importance of the team and the value of hard work. He was a big believer in the thought that when talent is roughly equal, the player or team that works harder will always come out on top. We had a lot of average players, but we practiced harder than most teams.

"Vice Admiral Edward C. Waller has established an award

for the Navy Lacrosse program which is presented each year to the midshipman who 'has contributed most to the spirit, morale, and well-being of the lacrosse team.' I believe that Admiral Waller, who was a multi-sport letterman during his midshipman days as well as the Superintendent later on, has shown great wisdom in establishing this award, very much like the Class of '32 from Hopkins. As an athlete and naval officer, he knew first hand how critical individual and group spirit and morale are to the mission of a unit.

"It is quite remarkable to me that in one of the letters Mr. Turnbull showed me from his brother, Jack mentioned that beyond his regular duties he was always concerned about the 'welfare and spirit of the team.' I was struck by how he used the term 'team' to describe his military unit. There is something to be learned from this individual and collective insight of two great military leaders."

Robbie was absorbing every word as he pounded the wall with his ball.

"Let's see, what else? I guess discipline is another aspect of the game that falls into this category. When we talk about discipline, we usually think of parents punishing their children. But in terms of team athletics, discipline means to play the way you practice and practice the way you play. I think that this is one of the most critical aspects of playing a team sport. Each player is obligated to conform to the guidelines set by the coach. There can really only be one vision for the team, and each player must accept that vision. It's not unlike doing battle in the military. In order for the team to 'win,' each person must do what he or she is trained and expected to do. Anything less can spell disaster. In Naval Aviation we had the phrase, 'train like you fight; fight like you train.'

"Discipline involves things like making good decisions under pressure, sticking to fundamentals when you get tired, not allowing yourself to let down when things get tough. I think that all of the other things I have mentioned before play into the concept of discipline. It is easy to say and difficult to execute. You often hear; 'Move your feet' or 'Get down' on ground balls and things of that nature. Well, they're all true and even more so when you get tired or things aren't going well for you or your team.

　"I've also found that talking doesn't make your team better. *Doing* does. The only groundball that matters is the next one. The only face-off that matters is the next one. We could say that about every aspect of the game.

"The key to being able to exercise discipline in games is to execute fundamentals repeatedly, correctly, and at full throttle in practice. So everything you do is either a good habit or a bad habit. How well and how hard you do things in practice will dictate how well you do them in games. So when your coaches bark about fundamentals and 'little things,' don't underestimate their significance. They almost always determine the outcome of a contest, and I have also seen the same in my experience as a naval officer.

"I think Mr. Turnbull would have said the same things about the game fifty years ago.

"So 'Respect the Game' takes many forms. Appreciating the history of the game, conditioning yourself physically and mentally, developing the skills of the game, sportsmanship, teamwork and team spirit, and discipline. That pretty much covers it. What do you think?"

"I think I understand it a little better now."

# Het Achterhuis

*I want to go on living even after my death.*
—Anne Frank

Red Hawk came to visit Robbie again on the next full moon.

"*Where would like to go this time, Robbie?*" Red Hawk asked.

"*Captain Lewis said that the meaning of the book,* Het Achterhuis (The Diary of Anne Frank), *would become clear to me. Can you help with that part of the story?*"

"*Sure. Let's go look.*"

*Red Hawk took Robbie to Lewis's home on Long Island on his sixteenth birthday, February 23, 1960. Doug Turnbull made it a point to visit Lewis on this day and had scheduled a business trip to the area. After dining with the family Turnbull was preparing to leave. The unseen guests looked on. As Doug reached the door, he turned to Lewis and handed him a book.*

"*Happy Birthday, Jim. I don't know how familiar you are with this book, but my mother gave it to me shortly after it was published in the United States in 1952. The title of the book literally means 'the house behind' referring to the 'secret annex' that Anne, her family, and another family occupied for more than two years. She asked me to read it and then the letter at the end. I'll ask you to do the same. Perhaps after you do so you'll understand why it's so important to me. It might be of some use to you.*" *With that Turnbull headed for his hotel.*

*A short while later, as Mr. Turnbull requested, Lewis began to read* Anne Frank, *dutifully planning to save the letter until he finished. Lewis, however, was not as patient to look for the diary entry on the day of his birth, Wednesday, February 23, 1944. He felt a rush of excitement as he found an entry for that special day. As he read it, he thought of the fact that the Holocaust had actually occurred during his lifetime. He read eagerly:*

> *The best remedy for those who are afraid, lonely, or unhappy is to go outside, somewhere where they can be quite alone with the heavens, nature, and God. Because only then does one feel that all is as it should be and that God wishes to see people happy, amidst the simple beauties of Nature. As long as this exists, and it certainly always will, I know that then there will always be comfort for every sorrow, whatever the circumstances should be. And I firmly believe that nature brings solace in all troubles....*
>
> *Riches can all be lost, but that happiness in your own heart can only be veiled, and it will still bring you happiness again, as long as you live. As long as you can look fearlessly up into the heavens, as long as you know that you are pure within, and that you will still find happiness.*

*At this point in his life Lewis hadn't given a great deal of thought to the majesty, mystery, and, yes, magic of nature, but he was certainly struck by the power and eloquence of this girl, who was nearly his age when she put her thoughts to paper. Spurred by this passage, Lewis began to contemplate the larger issues of Natural Law.*

*Red Hawk advanced the scene forward a week, after Lewis had completed reading the* Diary. *He and Robbie looked on as Lewis slipped the letter from its envelope and read:*

*August 18, 1952*

Douglas,

   *It's difficult to believe that it's been almost eight years since we lost Jack. At times it seems like yesterday and at others it seems like forever ago. I should start by saying that a mother can never completely reconcile the unspeakable pain of losing a son. I am no exception. Having to do so without your father has made it doubly difficult. I shall never be able to patch the gaping hole in my heart. I have always wanted to believe that Jack's loss, though, was justified in some way—specifically by helping to end the senseless, heinous, and widespread persecution of so many innocent people. This amazing book has put my heart at some ease, knowing that Jack and his crews, though unable to spare this brilliant young woman, may have prevented a similar loss of even one innocent young girl like her. I have finally achieved some solace.*

   *I know how much you already adore your children. But I hope that after reading this book you will be moved even more to cherish every single second you have with them—particularly your exquisite girls. I have copies of this book for each of your children. At their young ages they will likely not fully grasp the power of this work— but perhaps they will begin to learn something about the injustices of the world, and, despite reading of the worst aspects of human nature, they may still believe in hope, as young Anne did. I am sure that as they grow older, they will appreciate it as much as I do. It is nearly impossible to believe that such insight, wisdom, compassion, hope, and beauty resided in the heart and mind of a fifteen-year-old girl! We were fortunate to have had Jack for as long as we did. The poor father of this girl must be suffering infinitely more than we are.*

   *I simply cannot imagine the horrors that were being*

*perpetrated at the hands of the Nazis. My heart breaks for every single person who was "exterminated" simply because of race or religion! War hardly ever seems like the best solution to conflicts between people or nations. But in this case, I can't see that there was any other way to stop these unspeakable atrocities.*

*I know what the loss of Jack has meant to you. I know that you've carried your loss silently deep in your heart, unseen by most people. A mother can sense the pain of her children, and I know that you've suffered much more than you've shown. I know that your feeling of loss is as deep today as it was so many years ago in 1944. But I beg you to continue to carry only the memory of Jack's goodness and heroism. Don't carry the pain of his loss. Please continue to channel any of the hurt into something good as you have done so admirably over these last eight years.*

*I think of Jack and your father every day—as I know you do. But we continue to bear the obligation of living our lives for today and tomorrow, to love and help our children, and to retain hope in our futures.*

*I often think of the only request your father made of his children: that you give more to this country than you take. You've all done that so, so well, each in very different, but equally important, ways.*

*I couldn't be more proud of you and all that you've done. You are a truly special son, brother, father, and citizen. Your father would have been extremely proud of you.*

*All my love,*
*Mum*


*Red Hawk then took Robbie to the Turnbull home the day after Mum's funeral, July 16, 1957. After all of the guests had returned home, Doug finally had some time to himself. He sat in his den and began meticulously inscribing the shaft of the stick with a tribute to his mother and brother—a carving of the cover of* Het Achterhuis.

*"It took Doug about eight hours to do that carving," Red Hawk shared. "I hope that gives you some sense of the role of that book in the history of the stick, Robbie."*

Once again, Robbie shared the dream with his parents and recorded the visit in great detail in his journal.

# The Greatest Ever

*Give a boy a stick he can hold*
*Give a boy a ball he can toss*
*And you've given him something that's better than gold*
*The pleasure of playing lacrosse.*
—Attributed to
Douglas C. Turnbull, Jr.

Lewis met the Jones family for lunch at the Mount Washington Tavern in Baltimore. He had previously arranged for a special guest to meet them there. At exactly 12:00, Lewis led Robbie to an older gentleman and introduced him.

"Stewart, this is Robbie Jones."

"Hi, Robbie, I'm Stewart McLean. It's a pleasure to meet you."

Robbie's eyes lit up, as did his parents'.

"John, Catherine, Mary, this is Stewart McLean, Naval Academy Class of '48, the first recipient of the Turnbull Award."

"It's quite an honor to meet you, Mr. McLean," offered John Jones.

"Stewart, please. And the pleasure is mine."

"I suppose Jim has shared with you the nature of our relationship?" said Mary.

"He has, and it sounds like a truly remarkable one at that. I wasn't aware that Doug and Jack had passed down a stick to Jim and then to your son."

"I thought it would be fun to meet Stewart since he actually knew Jack and Doug and saw both of them play. Would you mind sharing a little bit of your relationship with the Turnbull brothers with Robbie and Catherine?" Lewis asked.

"Not at all. Well, it's been quite a while since anyone has asked me about those two men. They were truly special, as were their parents and sisters.

"I grew up not far from here in the Mount Washington part of town. I played lacrosse at St. Paul's School. After playing for Hopkins, both Doug and Jack played for the Mount Washington Club. For many years—decades, really—Mount Washington was the best team in the country. We idolized those guys. I was lucky because their field was only a five-minute walk from my house and a ten-minute walk from school. I got to see both of them play quite a bit. By then Doug was playing mostly defense. Jack played everywhere. He faced off and played attack. He was tenacious but fair in everything he did. They were fun to watch. They were always gentlemen on and off the field. We would talk to them after games, and they always took the time to throw around with us.

"Doug was the only four-time first-team All-America for fifty years. A player named Frank Urso from Maryland earned his fourth award in 1975. I remember reading that Doug presented the certificate to him. He was genuinely happy for the young man. Then another player from Hopkins, Del Dressel, accomplished it again in the mid-eighties. Doug worked for many years as an executive at the B&O Railroad here in Baltimore. He was always active in the game."

Lewis picked up the story, "Mr. Turnbull was inducted into the National Lacrosse Hall of Fame in 1962—the year I graduated from high school. Many people consider Doug to be the greatest player ever. If you ask him, though, he would be the first to tell you that Jack far surpassed his abilities. The only reason Jack wasn't also a four-time first-team All America was that he graduated in three years! So did Doug, by the way, but he kept playing while he worked on graduate studies. Had Jack used his fourth year, he certainly would have equaled Doug's accomplishment."

Lewis continued, "He often told me how he had used the stick religiously—throwing against his family's barn, working his skills and then working them some more. He decided to share the stick with his younger brother Jack—actually as a precocious four-year-old Jack had already helped himself to the stick. Doug didn't fight it because the stick created a special bond between the brothers.

"I was extremely fortunate to have had a forty-five-year correspondence—maybe two or three letters per year—with Mr. Turnbull that has made me who I am today. Well, two or three letters per year for forty-five years has turned into about 120 letters from him. Mr. Turnbull also sent me a book every year on my birthday. My parents were always grateful that he thought so well of me that he encouraged me to read. They were great books, too! The amazing thing is that he sent me a book every year until he died—not just when I was a kid or in school. So I have accumulated quite a library, more than forty books—actually, it's more like ninety because he sent me the set called *The Harvard Classics*, which includes about fifty volumes, on my graduation from college. Each book was specially selected by him, and he always inscribed a thoughtful and personal comment and an inspirational quotation in each. It's quite a collection of letters and books, which meant a lot to me at the time but obviously means even more to me the older I get.

"I learned a lot about the game of lacrosse. What its true spirit was and is. Mr. Turnbull was able to offer me advice about things in my life every step of the way. His role in my life has been incredible—and has very much made me who I am today. He was a truly great man."

McLean took his cue to continue.

"Robbie, did you know that Jack was a member of the United States Olympic Team?"

"No, sir," Robbie responded. Then he suddenly connected the figure of the Olympic rings.

"Did he do the carving of the rings on the stick?" he asked of Lewis.

"Yes, Robbie, he did. But I should add that he participated in *two* Olympic Games—one in lacrosse in 1932 when he captained the team that won the gold medal. He was also a member of the 1936 U.S. men's field hockey team which competed in Berlin, ironically in front of Hitler."

Everyone's eyes lit up.

"Robbie, I think if you look carefully at the carving on the stick, you'll see that there are actually two sets of rings, one superimposed upon the other," Lewis offered. "Jack carved one set after each Olympiad."

Robbie mentally confirmed the fact, "Yes, I thought it looked like two sets!"

McLean continued, "Robbie, if you have half as much fun as Jim and I had playing lacrosse, you'll be one lucky young man. I think Jim would agree that lacrosse has added something special to our lives. It has provided us with life-long bonds with our teammates and coaches and, in many cases, with some of our opponents as well. It is truly a special game." Lewis nodded.

After lunch, Lewis drove Robbie and his family to 2111 Sulgrave Avenue in the Mount Washington part of town and identified it as the Turnbull home. Robbie gazed in awe as Lewis stopped to extend their look. They continued on.

McLean met the family at the Lacrosse Museum and National Hall-of-Fame adjacent to The Johns Hopkins University's Homewood Field. Lewis walked the family to the field and gave them some sense of the history of Johns Hopkins lacrosse and his experience playing on the field.

"This is one of the most historic fields in the game of

lacrosse. Many people liken it to Yankee Stadium. Hopkins has won some forty-seven national championships in lacrosse. Playing at Navy-Marine Corps Memorial Stadium was always a thrill, but it was also an extraordinary privilege to play here. I'll never forget the game I played here in 1965 when we beat Hopkins in front of their Homecoming crowd of over 7,000. It was particularly special for me due to my relationship with Mr. Turnbull."

They walked back to the Museum. Lewis paused before the magnificent, life-size bronze sculpture gracing the front entrance. Stretching their sticks for a ball two Indians are frozen for all time.

Robbie stared at the statue, poring over the detail. He noticed the players wearing only breechclouts, moccasins, and war paint on their arms, legs, torsos, and faces. One of the players, the one with the ball in his stick, was jumping. Robbie wondered if the fact that one native had a left-handed stick while the other had a right-handed one was a coincidence. Probably not. He thought of Red Hawk playing the game in this fashion.

The boy read the inscription on the dedication plaque:

*DEHONTSHIHGWA'ES*
*(Creator's Game)*
*The game of lacrosse was given by the Creator to the*
*Ho-de-no-saunee (Iroquois) and other Native*
*American people many ages ago. It is from the Iroquois*
*that the modern game of lacrosse most directly*
*descends. May this sculpture forever honor the Iroquois*
*and the origins of Lacrosse.*
*Donated by Emil A. "Buzzy" Budnitz, Jr.*
*Lacrosse Hall-of-Fame Class of 1976*
*June 4, 1992*

Robbie's eyes lit up the instant he walked through the doors of the Museum. Lewis allowed the family to soak in the sights and sounds at their own pace. Robbie and his sister were particularly fascinated by the display case holding a variety of ancient sticks, all in different shapes and sizes, representing different tribes. They also saw the magnificent three-foot-high Turnbull Trophy, housed in its own case. Robbie craned his head to locate the names of Lewis and McLean. His heart jumped when he was able to get the right angle to read Lewis's.

When the parents saw Robbie fixated on the trophy, they came up behind and realized the significance of his gaze. Lewis offered, "Stewart is too modest to point this out, but that's his name inscribed on the top."

McLean proudly led the group to the Hall-of-Fame room, pausing at the entrance to point out the plaque dedicated to his Navy coach, William H. Moore:

> *The Lacrosse Hall-of-Fame room*
> *pays tribute to "Dinty" Moore*
> *who served as the first president of the Lacrosse*
> *Hall-of-Fame Foundation 1960-67...*
> *for his ongoing contribution to the preservation*
> *and promotion of the sport.*
> *This room serves as a legacy*
> *to his leadership and vision.*

McLean then pointed out the plaques of Moore and his high school coach, Howdy Myers, among the greats enshrined. "I was extremely fortunate to have such great coaches, Robbie. Oh, and let's not forget Captain Lewis," McLean concluded as he gestured toward the 1981 inductees.

John and Mary Jones were as enthralled with the museum as their children. Lewis and McLean patiently answered their questions which arose during the next two hours.

# Uncle Tom's Cabin

*It is rather for us to be here dedicated to the great task remaining before us—
that from these honored dead we take increased devotion to that cause for
which they gave the last full measure of devotion—that we here highly resolve
that these dead shall not have died in vain.*
—From Abraham Lincoln's "Gettysburg Address"

Upon falling asleep on the night of the next full moon,
Robbie was visited by Red Hawk.

*"Hi, Robbie."*

*"Hi."*

*"Well, have you had any thoughts since we spoke last time? Is
there anything you want to see now?"*

*"Would it be possible to learn anything about Mr. Turnbull's
relationship with the previous custodian?"*

*"Sure. Let's take a look."*

Red Hawk took Robbie for another trip through time. *"This is
Gettysburg National Military Park in May, 1913. The man you see
there,"* Red Hawk pointed, *"is General Joshua 'Lawrence'
Chamberlain, who led the Twentieth Maine in an historic Civil War
battle here in 1863."*

Red Hawk quietly narrated the solemn scene as Robbie watched
the old man, who sat on a large rock that held a granite monument
just off a trail at the bottom of Little Round Top. Robbie immediately
identified the figure on the monument next to Chamberlain as the
one on the shaft of the stick. He broke his silence, asking Red Hawk
in an excited whisper, *"Is that the same cross that's on the stick?"*

"Yes it is, Robbie. It's called the Maltese Cross—it's the symbol used to represent the Union troops. Chamberlain carved it into the shaft on his visit here on the twenty-fifth anniversary of the battle. I watched him do it. It took him most of the day to get it how he wanted it."

Another part of the puzzle solved, Robbie mused. They continued to watch.

Chamberlain sat lost in thought, whispering quietly to himself with a canteen lying by his side and holding the stickball stick gently in his now-feeble hands. He had performed this same ritual many times before. The general had just completed an extensive walk of the sacred grounds of the Battlefield, pondering the momentous battle that took place between the Army of Northern Virginia and the Army of the Potomac on July 2, 1863. He had visited the cemetery where, four months after the battle, President Lincoln delivered the "Gettysburg Address". He had also just visited the famous stone wall where the desperate Pickett's Charge ultimately withered, inches short of a possible Confederate victory—a victory that might well have earned the South secession in the War Between the States. Chamberlain had finally arrived here at the foot of Little Round Top, the true purpose of his trip.

Robbie and Red Hawk stood within hearing distance of the general and listened as he spoke to himself.

Chamberlain closed his eyes and replayed in his mind the heroics of his men—the 20th Maine Infantry Regiment—reliving the tremendous horror and ultimate triumph of that pivotal day nearly fifty years before. He thought of the men who had given their lives for a greater good—the unification of their country. Chamberlain's memory at age eighty-three recalled the events with all of the sights, sounds, smells, and emotions as fresh as if they were yesterday. The general fought back tears as he recalled the names and faces of every Maine man he had lost on that fateful day. As he conducted his heartbreaking roll call, he reminded himself of how fortunate he had been to lead those brave souls. He sat—in his earlier years he had knelt—for some 90 minutes, individually *honoring each man with a personal eulogy. It was the least he could do, he pined. They deserved so much more.*

*Red Hawk turned to his left, looking a few hundred yards toward the top of the narrow path, and briefed Robbie on the scene unfolding in that sector.*

*Doug Turnbull, Sr., and his son, ten-year-old Doug, Jr., had arrived at Gettysburg that spring day at about 10 a.m. The elder Turnbull was a well-read Civil War buff and the boy, like so many his age, was greatly intrigued by all things military. So the father and son had set off that morning from their home just north of Baltimore for a forty-five-mile day trip to the Battlefield.*

*That morning the senior Turnbull had observed Chamberlain making his rounds of the park. He told his son that the man looked like General Joshua Lawrence Chamberlain, the hero of Little Round Top. He had seen pictures of Chamberlain in newspapers and magazines. Doug, Sr. chose to honor the privacy of the general and simply walked the grounds with his son, admonishing the boy that they should keep their distance and allow the gentleman to have his time. The father shared some pertinent biographical informa-tion on the general with his son. He noted that during the war the general had been shot six times. The boy was overwhelmed by the presence of the general and begged his father to talk to him. Finally, the general rose from his pew among the rocks and boul-ders at the flank of Little Round Top. The Turnbull father and son stood nearly one hundred yards away, allowing the general all the privacy they felt he needed.*

*The senior Turnbull was particularly sensitive to what Chamberlain must have been feeling that day. As they observed the general from afar, Turnbull pondered the gloomy notion that Chamberlain might be suffering from the all-too-common melan-choly that befell so many other men and women as they approached major anniversaries in their lives. He knew that Chamberlain was three months short of the fiftieth anniversary of the battle. Turnbull couldn't help but consider the uncanny coincidence that called Thomas Jefferson and John Adams to their eternal rest fifty years to the day after they signed the Declaration of Independence. He thought of the countless others who had suffered a similar fate, family members who had died on or near such anniversary dates of their spouses, siblings, parents, and children. He knew Chamberlain must have been vulnerable to such melancholy feelings at this point. Turnbull hoped his fears were unfounded, but he had lived too long and seen too many such occurrences. He feared for the general.*

*To the astonishment and joy of the Turnbulls, Chamberlain began to walk slowly toward them. The visitors from Baltimore made eye contact with the hero, and the general said softly, "Good afternoon, gentlemen. What a great day for a walk."*

*"Yes, sir," Doug, Sr., replied.*

*"I am Lawrence Chamberlain," the general offered in a remarkably unassuming manner. Then with a little more voice, "And who do I have the honor of meeting this fine afternoon?" He looked directly at Doug, junior.*

*"Douglas Turnbull, senior and junior, General, and the honor is ours," replied the senior Turnbull.*

*Chamberlain caught the title General in the father's introduction, though he had carefully not offered that information. The father had obviously read at some length and depth on the Civil War, Chamberlain thought to himself, for he knew that he was surely not a household name—or face—anywhere outside Maine, if even there.*

*"And what brings you fine gentlemen here today?" the general asked.*

*"Just taking the boy on a trip to experience some history, sir"*

*"Are you an historian, my good man?"*

*"No, sir, but I've been greatly intrigued by the Civil War for as long as I can remember. My grandfather fought in this battle as part of the 44th New York Infantry. He survived the war but died suddenly shortly after my father was born in 1873. My father and the rest of his family have very little first-hand knowledge of the Civil War. They were far too busy just meeting their daily needs back then to think much about preserving or studying anything my grandfather had kept from that period. So I've tried to follow up*

on his service some. My boy is quite taken with it as well."

Turnbull's remark about his grandfather immediately stirred in Chamberlain the feeling that through the brotherhood of arms he was kin to these strangers.

"God bless your grandfather," Chamberlain proclaimed. "Was he a soldier or an officer?"

Conventional wisdom would have placed higher esteem in being able to respond 'officer,' but Turnbull had read enough to know how Chamberlain felt about his soldiers and he proudly replied, "Soldier, sir, an infantryman who advanced to sergeant by the end of the war."

"Magnificent! Ah, the soldiers, what great men. They never get near the credit they deserve. My compliments to your grandfather, my boy," Chamberlain beamed, still addressing the elder Turnbull.

"When we saw you this morning, sir, it struck me that you were perhaps General Chamberlain from the Twentieth Maine. Is that correct?" Turnbull posed, one-hundred percent sure that it was, else he would not dare be so bold.

"I am that man, sir. May I ask how you would know?"

"As I said, I've tried to study the war some, and I have seen your essays and articles as well as pictures of you in magazines and newspapers." Young Doug, who had been standing close by his father as still as a post, staring at the great hero, finally stirred.

"Is that a l-l-lacrosse stick that you are holding, sir?" the boy asked timidly.

"Well, I believe it is, young man! The man who gave me this stick called its game 'stickball' from the Cherokee, but I've heard the game referred to as lacrosse. Are you familiar with the game?"

"Yes, sir, I have a stick of my own at home!"

"Well, then there is a good chance that you know a lot more about the game than I do. A Confederate officer gave this stick to me very near to where we are right now."

The Turnbulls presented inquisitive looks, so Chamberlain continued, "It's quite a long story with which I will not burden you, but the officer was wounded and I saw to him. Later at the field hospital, he presented me with this stick. It was a noble gesture that I thought myself unworthy of at the time, nor am I sure that I am worthy today. I carry it with me every time I come here. It helps me regain the vision of that day."

The father asked about the upcoming fiftieth anniversary reunion. Chamberlain shared that the objective of his present trip was to represent his state of Maine at the conference to plan the reunion. Most of the officials were to arrive the next day, he explained. He had arrived early to enjoy peace on the field alone. Tomorrow would be far too hectic. For the next hour or so, the general was most gracious, fielding and asking questions of the man and boy.

"I plan to be here for the big event on July 1," Chamberlain announced. "I would very much like to meet you here at that time, but I fear that there will be as many as 50,000 veterans, camped all around. I would not recommend this event for the public. It will be a solemn occasion for the veterans and of little use to the general population. Oh, I'm sure there will be many others here for it, including the newspapers, but it really is for the soldiers. However, if you'd like to attend, I'll be sure to have some time with you. I'll allow you to decide.

"I make a trip here most years, or at least I did until my wife passed away in 1905, the 18th of October to be exact. Since then this is my first return. Before that, we visited every year or two. Perhaps I could meet you here again next summer and, in the meantime, if you wish we can continue our acquaintance through the mail. Here is my address. If you will forgive me, my good men, I should be leaving for my lodging now. These old legs aren't what they used to be." The father and son excused the general and stood spellbound as Chamberlain slowly departed.

Red Hawk then conveyed to Robbie the nature of the correspondence between the Turnbulls and the general over the next several months.

"The first letter was to Chamberlain from the elder Turnbull, thanking him for his graciousness and informing him of his incred-

*ible impact upon the boy," Red Hawk explained.*

*"A few weeks later Chamberlain sent a telegram to the family announcing his regret that his ill health would prevent him from attending the fiftieth anniversary celebration, after all. This news caused the senior Turnbull to rekindle his grave concerns for the general's health.*

*"Chamberlain's old wound from Petersburg finally betrayed him in the fall of 1913, causing him to be bedridden for most of the winter. He passed away on the morning of February 24, 1914. Doug Turnbull senior read of the general's death in the* Washington Post *the following day and broke the sad news to the boy. Fortunately, since the telegram of the previous summer the father had been preparing the boy. He knew that several historians believed that Chamberlain was the only soldier still suffering from his war wounds. Fifty years later all of the others had succumbed. He had beaten the odds, Turnbull reasoned, and the infinite satisfaction of having survived the fifty years made Chamberlain particularly vulnerable. Turnbull had begun to prepare the boy."*

Red Hawk then took Robbie to the Turnbull home in Baltimore on the morning of February 28, 1914. Just as Robbie and Red Hawk arrived at their station, a package arrived at the door addressed to the elder Turnbull. The return address was "J.L. Chamberlain, Brunswick, Maine." The father was quite alarmed to see such a return address and quickly opened the letter on the outside of the box. It read:

*February 12, 1914*

*Dear Mr. Turnbull,*

*I have asked my daughter Daisy to prepare this letter and box for shipment upon the arrival of my imminent death. It is a gift from me to your fine son. I would ask you to speak with him before he opens the box, with the hope that you might be able to explain the nature of death to him...*

*With Warmest Regards and Thanks,*

*J.L. Chamberlain*

*The elder Turnbull obliged Chamberlain's request by speaking to the boy about the death of the general and sharing his views on life, death, and heaven. He then handed the boy the box.*

*The boy opened the box and found inside it a letter from the general, an old leather bag containing the stick he had carried with him at Getttysburg with a small ball tucked away at the bottom, and in a wooden jewelry box a copy of the book* Uncle Tom's Cabin *by Harriet Beecher Stowe. In the hand of Chamberlain's daughter, the letter read:*

*February 12, 1914*

*Dear Doug,*

*Please accept these gifts as a token of my esteem for you and your father. The afternoon that we spent at Gettysburg was most splendid.*

*I send you these two gifts—both of which have meant so much to me over these many years—to help you understand some of the ways of the world at your young age. You may have read the magnificent work by Mrs. Stowe. If you have not, I commend its reading at your earliest convenience. You will note the message inside the front cover. Mrs. Stowe was the wife of one of my professors at Bowdoin. The Stowes would frequently entertain students in their home on Saturday evenings for scholarly discussion and readings. I was fortunate to have been included in those gatherings. She was a most brilliant, devout, passionate, and compassionate woman.*

*Doug quickly opened the front cover and saw the message:*
*Lawrence,*

*What a delight to get to know you during this unforgettable year. My gratitude for your warm reception of this story.*

*May the Good Lord find a way to make use of your
unbounded Intellect, Spirit, and Character in easing the
plight of these desperate people.*

*Congratulations on your Commencement from
Bowdoin College.*

*Godspeed,*
*Harriet Beecher Stowe*
*June 12, 1852*

Doug marveled at the book, not realizing the significance of a
sixty-year-old signed first edition. He would read it in short order,
he told himself. He continued on with the letter:

*The stick I send as well, mostly because it represents
so much that is good in man, even at the worst of times.
As I told you last year, this stick was presented to me at
the field hospital behind the Union lines at Gettysburg.
I shall not dwell on my own actions during the fray, nor
will I subject my daughter to recording the incident.*

*I can speak to the stick itself, however. Since the stick
was presented to me as an act of kindness between two
combatants, I have held it in the highest regard for the last
fifty years. It is sufficient to say that the Confederate
officer, Col. Casey, asked me to pass the stick along to a
worthy young man of my choosing in the name of honor
and compassion. I believe you will find the stick will aid
you in learning about the proud people whence it came.*

*I trust you will treat this gift with the respect it has
earned over the last one-hundred-plus years. At a place and
time of your choosing, please pass it along to another
worthy young man.*

*May God Bless You,*
*J.L. Chamberlain*

*Robbie looked in amazement at Chamberlain's pained signature. He turned to Red Hawk, "So that's how the stick and book were passed down?"*

*"Yes. A pretty remarkable story, isn't it?"*

Robbie shared the details of his dream with his parents who asked him to record it in his journal.

# Always Be a Gentleman!

*To read well, that is, to read true books in a true spirit, is a noble exercise, and one that will task the reader more than any exercise which the customs of the day esteem. It requires a training such as the athletes underwent, the steady intention almost of the whole life to this object.*
—Henry David Thoreau
*Walden*

Robbie received an e-mail from Captain Lewis reading:

Robbie, I'm sorry that I cannot make a trip to see you this month as I had planned. Please forgive me. We just picked up a project which is going to require me to be in the office almost non-stop for about two weeks. I had been meaning to share this letter that I received from Mr. Turnbull on the occasion of my high school graduation. I found it very useful at the time and I have read it many times since. I'll call you in a few weeks.

Robbie responded, "No problem. THANKS," and eagerly opened the attachment:

June 22, 1962

Dear Jim,

Today you reach a significant milestone in your life, your graduation from high school. I thought I'd take a minute to share a few thoughts with you as you prepare to take a new path in your life.

First of all, I hope that you realize how much I have enjoyed our relationship over the last four years. I hope that your growth as custodian of Red Hawk's stick has been as great and rewarding as mine.

I cannot begin to share the countless lessons I have learned from Red Hawk and the stick. You will surely benefit from the stick as I did, but you will also benefit from your own explorations and experiences, and from a number of people that you will meet along the way.

Your choice of college presents a unique challenge that will affect everything you do in your life from here forward. I commend and thank you for "picking up where Jack Turnbull left off." Your tribute to Jack and our family, not to mention our country, is truly humbling.

Though I was never a military officer, perhaps I can offer some of Jack's insight for your consideration. Jack was always first and foremost concerned for his men. He always made sure that their needs were met before he considered anything for himself. That included his junior officers—not just his enlisted men. Next to that, Jack placed a high priority on physical strength and courage. He never let anyone in the chain-of-command outwork him physically.

Jack expected a lot from his men. He got their best efforts because he was fair with them. They appreciated his skill, knowledge, ability, and work ethic, but he gained their respect because he genuinely cared about them and worked hard for them.

When the men let Jack, themselves, or the crew down, he made sure to identify the deficiency, but he did it in a positive manner. He always found ways for the men to remedy and improve the situation. As you assume your positions of leadership in the fleet in a few years, I hope that Jack's example might be of some use to you.

At this point in my life, I have sometimes looked back to see what I have learned. Though I feel I have learned a great deal, I often tell my children that I am still not much closer to knowing what I would like to know—or even what I need to know. I think a lot about the ways of the world, and what might be called the "Laws of Nature."

So let me "think on paper" a little and share some of those reflections, with the hope that you accept these musings not as absolute truth, but rather as a starting point from which to begin thinking about issues, taking your own journey, and if you are lucky, arriving at your own conclusions. So, with fifty-nine years behind me, here are a few thoughts:

I can never read enough!

I have come to believe that patience is the greatest of all virtues.

I have become infinitely more appreciative of the intrinsic, aesthetic value of art, music, poetry, theater, dance, and literature over the years.

I have come to believe that actions are worth far more than words—and its corollary that the best form of leadership is example.

I have learned that substance is worth a lot more than style, that function is worth a lot more than form, and that good friends are worth a lot more than money.

I have learned the value of taking advantage of one's opportunities.

I have become much more sensitive to the precarious balance of nature. I try not to consume or waste any more that I absolutely have to.

I have endeavored to study history so that I might learn more about the human condition. I have found that life has always been a struggle and always will be.

I think since Jack's death I have tried not to take anything for granted—my health, my wife, my children, my job. As you know, within a few weeks of each other just a few years ago, my mother passed away, and my son graduated from West Point. Both events brought into even sharper focus the fragility and uncertainty of our lives. I have developed a tremendous appreciation for life. I feel fortunate to have had such positive support from my family and friends all these years, but especially to have my children as healthy as they are. I don't know what the future holds for my son Bruce, now a first lieutenant in the U.S. Army. All I can do is hope that he works hard and that he will answer the calls put to him. As his father, though, I have to admit that I secretly pray that he will not be called as Jack was.

I have become painfully aware that Thomas Paine's maxim, "Those who expect to reap the blessings of liberty must undergo the fatigues of supporting it," is so true. My mother, in particular, bore that burden during World War II. As our son wears the uniform of the United States, my wife and I go to sleep every night bearing those very same "fatigues" of supporting our country's freedom. Your parents will, as well.

I regret to inform you that your will, courage, honor, integrity, fidelity, strength, resilience, and intellect will be challenged beyond what they have been at this point, and at times more than you will want. My only advice in this area is to work hard, and remember that maintaining your honor in difficult times can never be bad. Perhaps Shakespeare's missive, "This above all, to thine own self be true," might guide you through particularly trying circumstances.

I have intentionally selected *Profiles in Courage* for your graduation gift. It seems an appropriate gift for a future leader. Please enjoy it.

So, Jim, congratulations on your graduation and best of luck as you engage a whole new world of challenges at the United States Naval Academy. I look forward to following your already-brilliant career on the lacrosse field. I hope to attend many games. You can count on me to be your biggest fan (except when you play Johns Hopkins!).

As always, please let me know if there is anything I can do to assist you. I know that Red Hawk will provide you a great deal of insight and wisdom.

Let me leave you with a saying that my father used to drill into Jack and me, "ABAG!" —Always Be a Gentleman!

Godspeed,
Doug

Once again, Robbie was overwhelmed by this heartfelt letter and shared it with his parents.

# The Greatest Love of Mankind

*General, you have the soul of a lion and the heart of a woman.*
—General Horatio G. Sickel
Describing Gen. J.L. Chamberlain
At the Quaker Road, Virginia, 29 MAR 1865

At the next full moon Red Hawk again appeared to Robbie.

*"Hi, Robbie. Is there anything you would like to see or a place you would like to go to tonight?"*

*"General Chamberlain never really said exactly how he met Colonel Casey at Gettysburg. I've been curious about that, you know, since they were on opposite sides. Do you know anything about that? Can we go there?"*

*Red Hawk brought Robbie to the slope of Little Round Top on July 2, 1863 as the Twentieth Maine and the Fifteenth Alabama prepared to clash. Red Hawk paused and cautioned Robbie that at this point they were about to observe actual battle but assured him that they would remain untouched by the action. He asked if the boy felt strong enough to witness the engagement. Robbie indicated his readiness. Red Hawk began with a brief description of what they were about to see.*

*"Casey was tasked with leading the 15th Alabama on an assault on the Union left flank at this location known as Little Round Top. Success in this venture likely would have allowed the Confederates to get behind the Union lines and claim victory. Failure to gain the flank would likely result in defeat! The sector was defended by the 20th Maine Infantry, commanded by then-Colonel Chamberlain.*

"After a long forced march, and with no water, Casey and his men made a daring and gallant charge—uphill—to take the flank. Both sides fought viciously and fearlessly. Despite the heroic efforts of his men Chamberlain saw the Confederates continue their charge. With his men nearly out of ammunition, he ordered his troops to fix bayonets and charge the rebels. This was an unorthodox and bold move to say the least.

"At this point the battle could have gone to either side. In fact, many people believe the disposition of the whole war hung in the balance during those fateful minutes on the slope of Little Round Top. Casey was wounded during the fray, hit in the leg by a bullet. Despite his terrible bleeding he continued with his men in their charge.

"Are you sure you're ready, Robbie?"

The boy nodded.

Despite his assent, Robbie was stunned to be thrown into the fray and was immediately overwhelmed by the action. The heat and smell nauseated him as did the ear-shattering noise. He saw dead and bloodied bodies all about and heard the visceral cries of those in their last moments of life. But he stood tall, comforted by the confidence that Red Hawk had brought him there to observe, not to participate.

The scene began as the injured Casey led the charge up the slope. He finally stumbled and fell just short of Chamberlain. The Confederate colonel aimed his pistol at Chamberlain, who was brandishing only his officer's saber. Just as Casey triggered his piece, Chamberlain instinctively dove to the ground and rolled toward the crippled southerner. He came out of his roll with his sword swinging toward the helpless officer. Chamberlain arrested his rage-filled swing when he sensed that the man he was about to kill was seriously wounded. Chamberlain rested his saber just below Casey's chin then slowly withdrew and sheathed it. The Union colonel immediately removed his neckerchief and applied it to Casey's gushing wound. Chamberlain summoned his medics to treat the officer. The men obliged, dragging Casey out of the fray *and laying him next to a tree where they could more carefully treat his wound.*

Red Hawk continued his description: "After Chamberlain had summoned his medics to treat Casey, he immediately returned to the carnage, leading his men in a stand to hold Little Round Top.

"Then after a brief rest, the 20th Maine was ordered as a support unit at Great Round Top. Chamberlain had been wounded in the foot at Little Round Top but chose to delay treatment while his men were still in reserve. His men helped repel the famous Pickett's Charge, and the Union line held. Only after the rebels began their retreat did Chamberlain report to the field hospital to tend to his wounds. When he arrived he specifically asked to see the Confederate colonel."

Red Hawk then took Robbie to the field hospital where Casey had been drifting in and out of consciousness all afternoon because of the tremendous loss of blood. As Chamberlain approached, limping badly, Casey identified him as the officer who had not only spared his life, but had saved it. Casey was grateful for the opportunity to thank the Union officer. The Alabaman extended his right hand, still shaking badly from the effects of shock. Chamberlain accepted the hand and held it firmly to ease its trembling.

"Colonel Patrick John Casey 15th Alabama, sir. You are wounded. You must be treated," Casey pleaded.

"Colonel Lawrence Chamberlain, 20th Maine. I'll be fine," the northerner replied calmly.

Not knowing if and how long he might live, Casey labored haltingly: "You, sir, spared then saved my life when you could easily and justifiably have ended it in the name of your cause. You have demonstrated the most remarkable display of honor and compassion man has ever witnessed."

"There has been more than enough death in this conflict already, my good man. I am sure that you would have done the same. Please rest."

Casey motioned to a medic to bring his pack. During every

*step of the campaign Casey had carried the bag and its precious contents with him, and it had provided him strength and wisdom. Casey's mind drifted back to the scene when he had received the stick twenty five years before. It seemed yesterday to him.*

*Casey handed the stick and bag to Chamberlain and continued his laborious comments, "For a man to spare the life of an enemy at great peril to himself is to have shown the greatest love of mankind. You, sir, are the epitome of nobility. This gift is in honor of your magnanimity. I hope it will serve you as well as it has served me. Godspeed. Now, please tend to your wounds."*

*Chamberlain squeezed the colonel's hand one last time and, despite a tremendous desire to stay to comfort the confederate, he obliged the request to seek treatment for his own wounds. He had already tempted fate in his delay. As Chamberlain was assisted to the Union tent, he prayed that the colonel would survive.*

*Robbie watched the exchange between the two colonels. For the first time in his life, ground combat had a face. At his young age, his schooling had provided only superficial details of battle, mostly names and dates. These were real people with real wounds and real feelings, Robbie thought. He was deeply moved by the heroic and noble actions of both officers.*

Robbie woke with a new-found energy. He made some remarks in his journal before he headed out to school and elaborated on them later that night.

# Name. Rank. Division.

*Rest on, embalmed and sainted dead,*
*Dear as the blood ye gave,*
*No impious footstep here shall tread*
*The herbage of your grave.*
*Nor shall your glory be forgot*
*While fame her record keeps,*
*For honor points the hallowed spot*
*Where valor proudly sleeps.*
—From "The Bivouac of the Dead"
Theodore O'Hara, 1847

Lewis met Robbie and his family at the visitor's center at Gettysburg National Military Park at the appointed time of 8 a.m. on March 10th. The group sat briefly for doughnuts, coffee, and drinks before embarking upon the ambitious task of the day—to cover as much of the Battlefield and Cemetery as possible before heading to Johns Hopkins to watch the Blue Jays' season opener versus Princeton.

"Robbie couldn't wait to meet you here today, Jim," John Jones said as his welcome.

"I thought this would be a good place to visit. Robbie has probably gained some sense of the significance of this Battlefield, but I thought it might be useful for all of us to visit here together. There's a lot to see. Mr. Turnbull met me and my parents here in 1962 before I entered the Naval Academy. He showed us the spot where he had met General Chamberlain in 1913. He also took me to the site of the make-shift field hospital. It has stayed in my mind ever since."

Lewis drove the family first to Little Round Top. He parked the car and allowed the family to mill around to take in the sight for a few minutes. Lewis drifted away down the slope.

"Well, this is where it happened," Lewis said as he stood on the steeply sloped hill. The family picked their way through the rocks to meet him.

"This is where Chamberlain and Casey met face-to-face. If Casey's shot had hit Chamberlain, there is a good chance none of us would be here."

The group stood quietly for several minutes, surveying the terrain and picturing in their own ways what must have happened here. Robbie could not believe the correspondence between his vision and the actual landscape.

Lewis then led them back up the hill and down a narrow walk—away from the main battle area and a number of impressive monuments—to the modest 20th Maine Monument.

"This is where Mr. Turnbull met Chamberlain," Lewis offered, looking at Robbie for confirmation of the exact location. Robbie nodded. The family noticed the Maltese Cross emblazoned on the sides of the cubic granite marker. Robbie's mind went back to the visit with Red Hawk—how they had watched Chamberlain sit there. Lewis then escorted the group back to the main area on Little Round Top, suggesting that the family peruse the grounds for themselves.

The sheer number of markers, statues, and historical plaques was enough to capture the attention of the guests for over an hour. Lewis smiled as he watched Robbie and Catherine struggle through the cracks and crevices of the rocky terrain while the parents contented themselves largely with the plaques and statues on the main walk.

John and Mary Jones read the marker honoring Colonel Strong Vincent's famous order to Chamberlain, "Hold this ground at all costs." Lewis gently whispered over their shoulders, "I think it is fair to say that any less an order may have caused Chamberlain to rethink his tactics. He really had no choice but to do what he did. Vincent died in the engagement."

Catherine and Robbie marveled at the life-size statues of the famous combatants. The group walked several hundred yards to the north and east. Again Lewis's eyes solicited Robbie's concurrence as he announced their arrival at the location of the field hospital. "This is where the actual exchange of the stick took place." The parents contemplated the circumstances occurring one-hundred and forty years before that had so dramatically affected their lives. A chill ran through them.

Lewis collected the group and drove them next to the wall made famous by imposing the ultimate failure of Pickett's Charge. Again the group was struck by the countless markers along the way and at the site. The larger-than-life bronze statue to General George Meade on horseback not far from the wall drew the family's attention. Virtually every regiment that fought had erected some tribute to their fallen comrades.

They walked to The Soldiers National Cemetery at Gettysburg. "Has Red Hawk brought you here yet, Robbie?" Lewis asked.

"No, sir."

"This might be the most compelling part of the whole park. This cemetery is located pretty near where the center of the Union line was positioned during the battle."

They walked to the large statue of Abraham Lincoln and read the words of the "Gettysburg Address" that he had presented as part of the dedication ceremony November 19, 1863. Next, they walked solemnly to the area where the Union soldiers were buried. Laid out in a semicircle around the centerpiece of the Cemetery—the magnificent Statue of Freedom—were 3512 gravestones, 979 of which were simply marked "unknown." The austerity of the markers struck

Robbie and his family—small granite stones. Name. Rank. Division. There was no separation between officers and soldiers. Each state was arranged together. Mary Jones was particularly pained to see the markers for the unknown soldiers. She silently pined over the mothers, the wives, the children, the families who never achieved closure.

As the group walked through the cemetery, Lewis pointed out the New York statue, looming high above their heads, commemorating the state that suffered the most severe losses. Lewis offered little commentary at this point and allowed the sights—and the assorted stanzas from the poem "The Bivouac of the Dead" spaced at equal intervals along the road—to speak for themselves.

Lewis then told Robbie and Catherine a story of his visit to this park with Doug Turnbull. "Mr. Turnbull shared with me that as beautiful, magnificent, compelling, and important as these monuments are, he was concerned that they might actually render a *disservice* to these heroic men."

The children stared at Lewis with inquisitive looks.

"Mr. Turnbull believed that a statue could never replace an actual person. That to reduce such brilliant lives to cold, unfeeling, inert masses can lead one to forget the spirit, energy, and life of these men. The artists commissioned to craft these pieces have an obligation to convey—somehow—these very traits. And as brilliant as they are, he thought they tell only a tiny fraction of the story. He told me that having his brother Jack back would have been worth more than a million statues.

"So as you look at each of these markers and monuments, try to remember that each of these men was a son, brother, husband, father. A real person with a smile, a wit, a spirit, a life all his own—gifts each shared with families, friends, communities, and comrades.

"Mr. Turnbull made a compelling case that it is up to those left behind to keep the memories of their fallen comrades alive. I have since lost many friends, colleagues, and shipmates. I have seen them remembered in a number of ways—tributes roughly similar to these at the United States Naval Academy, as well as many other places. I have tried very hard, though, not to let the lives of my friends be reduced to marble or bronze. I have actively tried to keep their spirits alive in what I do, to keep them alive in my heart and mind, to share their goodness—what they have given me—with as many people as I can. I try to live the example these people have provided me. Each of these markers has inspired me to give a little more, to be a little more patient, and to be a better person."

The children began to understand Lewis's point.

"Well, I guess that's about it for now. 51,000 killed, wounded, or captured. Not much else to say.

"We need to be leaving soon if we want to get to Johns Hopkins on time. There's a pre-game ceremony which I think you'll like to see."

Lewis made sure that his guests were seated and prepared for what they were about to see. Most of the other spectators were remarkably subdued a full fifteen minutes before game time. It was the first home game of the season for the Blue Jays, and the sophisticated followers of the program knew that reverence and quiet was in order.

"Ladies and gentlemen, at this time we ask that you please stand for the Annual Memorial Ceremony," the public address announcer began. The 8,000 fans directed their attention to the Hopkins team captains standing on the midfield line in front of their team's bench. As each of the two players began walking solemnly toward opposite goals, the announcer continued, "For 82 years, at each home game of the Johns Hopkins University, there has hung at one goal a service flag with three gold stars. That flag, presented by the lacrosse team of 1919, commemorates the loss in World War I of three Hopkins lacrosse players. These men are:

W. Brown Baxley
Warren B. Hunting
And Theodore Prince.

"A second service flag bears eight gold stars which pay tribute to eight former Hopkins lacrosse players who lost their lives in the Second World War and in the Vietnam War.

"From World War II, they are:

Frank Cone
Walter J. Farenholz
David H. W. Houck
George D. Penniman III
Edward A. Marshall
Peter W. Reynolds
And John I. Turnbull.

"And in the Vietnam War:

Charles E. Aronhalt.

"We pause today to rededicate the flag of World War I and the flag of World War II and the Vietnam War. These flags will always hang in the goals at each home game of the Johns Hopkins University lacrosse team.

"Please remain standing until these flags are attached to the goals."

Lewis and the Joneses stood unfazed by the biting March wind, absorbed by the solemnity of the ceremony. The length and *depth* of the silence shook the first-time observers as all in attendance patiently observed the captains perform their time-honored duty. The captain nearest the Lewis's group paused as he arrived behind the goal, took an exaggerated breath, stared at his flag momentarily, and knelt next to the goal as if before an altar. Mary Jones's knees buckled in sympathy with the player's as he assumed his position. The captain carefully weaved the strings of the flag into the stringing of the net.

The only noises Robbie heard were the steady whistling of the wind and the sharp cracking of the American flag flying above the stadium. Then his ear picked up the muffled tone from the goal near him. Though not nearly as loud, the service flag had begun to sing the same song as the Stars and Stripes above. As Robbie stared at the service flag he was shaken by the thought that one of the stars represented the life of Jack Turnbull. He watched the stars gently undulate in response to the wind. The boy felt as though the wind—maybe it was Jack—was talking to him.

The captains made their way to the sideline and the warm welcome of their teammates and coaches. The visiting Princeton Tigers rendered their respect with soft applause for the captains.

"Thank you," the public address announcer concluded.

As the teams gathered for final coaching instructions and team cheers, the crowd sat and began to buzz with excitement for the impending season-opening faceoff. Lewis leaned closer to Robbie and whispered above the wind, "Robbie, I played against the last player they mentioned—Chuck Aronhalt. He was Class of '64 here at Hopkins, so I played against him when he was a senior and I was a sophomore. I knew Chuck had died in Vietnam in 1967 so I called Hopkins a few weeks ago to get some information about this ceremony and Chuck. They sent me everything they had. I read all of the records on Chuck's actions in the battle in which he was killed, and let me just say that he took actions to protect his men at the expense of his own life. There is no greater service that anyone can provide for another or for his country. Chuck had already been awarded the Bronze Star for heroism in *another* engagement and then was awarded the

Distinguished Service Cross—the second highest award for heroism behind the Congressional Medal of Honor—for the valiant actions that cost him his life. Chuck also played football here and was captain of the team as a senior. The football team has presented an award in Chuck's honor and memory since he passed away. I remember him hitting me pretty hard a few times when we played in Annapolis in 1964! We still beat them, though, 15-3, I think," Lewis concluded with a smile.

"O.K. should we watch the game? Remember when you asked me what it's like to play college lacrosse? Well, this is it right here. These two teams are about as good as you'll see. You already know quite a bit about Hopkins, but Princeton is fantastic also. This should be a great game. Just watch how skilled these guys are and how hard they play. See what you can learn from them. It should be fun—and you should get some sense of how much I enjoyed it!"

True to Lewis's prediction, the game was a hard-fought battle with excellent play by both teams for the entire sixty minutes.

# The Greatest Gift

*Without hope, we are all lost.*
—Kofi Annan
Secretary-General of the United Nations

Red Hawk did not appear to Robbie again for another twenty-eight days, till the next full moon.

*"Hi, Robbie. Is there anything you'd like to do tonight?"*

"Well, last time you mentioned Colonel Casey. Was that his name? Can you tell me how he got the stick?"

*"Sure, but I must warn you that some of the scenes in this part of the story are also difficult to witness. Do you think you can do it?"*

"I'll try," Robbie replied uneasily.

*"Well, let me ask you this. Do you know anything about the Trail of Tears?*

"No, I don't think so."

*"Well, when I was seventeen, our entire Nation was driven off our native grounds by the United States government."*

*Robbie immediately felt uncomfortable with the discussion, sensing the injustice toward Red Hawk and his people.*

*Red Hawk continued, "The first part of the process was for the soldiers to round us up and get us into their stockades with no regard for our property or families. So they took us at the end of their rifles, poking stragglers with their bayonets. As I was being forced from my family's cabin I was able to grab a bag my grand-*

*father had given me with the sticks and some of my sister's clothes. I thought as I grabbed the sticks that my grandfather's spirit would help get my sister and me through whatever was about to happen. The soldiers got me, my sister, and my mother on a wagon. My father was way off in our field. He raced back a short time after we were carted off, but fortunately we were able to be reunited at the same stockade. Many other families were torn apart."*

*Robbie felt himself growing sick at the injustice and pain and wasn't sure whether he wanted to hear the rest. Red Hawk saw the change in Robbie's countenance and asked if he should stop.*

*"No, please go on," Robbie said reluctantly.*

*"I don't have to, Robbie."*

*"No—I want to learn about the stick and your people."*

*Red Hawk decided to edit out some of the more gruesome aspects of the horror, particularly the parts describing soldiers' stealing, extortion, and the unspeakable liberties many took with the women and girls. Robbie wasn't ready for all of that, Red Hawk realized.*

*"Well, my mother died of cholera in the holding pen."*

*Robbie felt tears well up in his eye. How could this have happened?*

*"My father and uncle died when the raft we were on with several others sank in the icy Ohio River. Somehow my sister and I managed to make it to shore. I believed then and I believe now that my grandfather's spirit was with us, and saved us."*

*Robbie could not believe what he was hearing.*

*"Lieutenant Casey was, at times, the only thing that kept us going. When my mother died in the stockade, he diverted from his orders by allowing me and my father outside the gate to bury her. On the Trail he came by to check on us when he could. After my father and uncle died in the river, Lieutenant Casey went even further out of his way to see that my sister and I were faring as well as could be expected. We were not the only ones who benefited from his goodness. Whenever he could he went out of his way to help us. My people had built up a great deal of contempt for the*

*officers and soldiers who drove them west. The soldiers were not particularly sympathetic. They simply continued to prod us with little regard for the well-being of our people. I regret to say that it was probably the best they could do as they had little food, water, and provisions themselves.*

*"Lieutenant Casey showed a great deal of empathy for me, my sister, and many others. He helped push our wagons out of the mud, rather than simply watching us do it ourselves. Instead of drinking water first, like most of his comrades, he made sure that the weak and elderly had an adequate amount. Instead of leaving the sick on the side of the road to die, Casey sought medical assistance whenever he could. Many times he even stayed behind to help bury the dead.*

*"We could see that Casey had been regularly chided by his superiors and even mocked behind his back by other soldiers for what they believed was diminishing himself to a level below his station. We knew that the lieutenant would be unable to relieve all our suffering, but he made the pain more bearable. He became a hero to everyone he helped, and for the rest of their lives those people would remember his acts of kindness."*

*Robbie was thankful for something positive in all of the misery.*

*"As my sister and I trudged along, day after day I quietly kept begging my grandfather to 'Stay with me.' Every day I became weaker and more heartsick, but I knew that I must go on, if for no other reason than to care for my sister. I think that if Lieutenant Casey had not helped us, we would have perished as well. For beyond the physical needs he met—a little food, some water, a blanket—it was the glimmer of hope he continued to keep alive in my heart that kept me going.*

*"I had nothing to offer Casey to repay his kindness. He gave us our lives. When we arrived in the Indian Territory after four miserable months, I wanted to thank him for the respect, character, and dignity he had worked so desperately to retain for all of my people.*

*"Then I saw a vision of my grandfather, who suggested that I*

present Casey with one of the sticks. I could almost feel my grand-father choosing the words as they came out of my mouth to Casey:

My grandfather presented this stick to me when I was a boy. It had been crafted for him by his grandfather many years before. He shared with me many of the lessons he believed would carry me through a difficult life. He also shared with me the spirit of the warrior and the spirit of our game. He died a short time later. Since he has passed to the Great Spirit, I have been able to feel his spirit in the stick, and I have even been able to communicate with him through it. He is always with me. When my mother, father, and other family members died during this dreaded march, my grandfather became my strength. Whenever I was in need, I invoked his spirit. I want you to have this stick because you have shown great character, empathy, and compassion. During the march your honor and courage were not overlooked. My people will always be heart-sick for having been driven from their homes. But it would be of no use for me, you, or our people to live in anger. Though many of my people will mock and ridicule me for retaining hope despite this unthinkable tragedy, just as you sometimes bore such rebuke for your humane efforts, you give me hope, the greatest gift one can offer, that our people might still be able to live together in harmony. Please keep this stick as a reminder of the great heritage of my people, and continue to be upright in all of your dealings with them. Perhaps when you are in need of assistance, you might solicit my grandfather's spirit to stay with you.

"After my sister and I survived the crossing of the Ohio River, I carved a Sunflower in the shafts of the sticks so that she would be with me for all time. We will keep the other stick and pass it down to our descendants, should we be so fortunate. You and I will be forever linked as individuals and as a people by these sticks. All I ask is that you continue to respect my people and all people.

"Respect the game of the Creator that means so much to us. Of all the things that were stripped from us in the removal, we will be able to maintain the dignity of our game. Pass the stick along to a worthy person of your choosing. Like you he should be a person of strength, spirit, character, leadership, courage, empathy, and compassion. I hope, he, like you and I, will feel the spirit in the stick and use that strength to the betterment of all people."

"I'm so sorry that you and your people were treated so badly, Red Hawk," Robbie offered sincerely.

"Thank you. Lieutenant Casey made it much more tolerable. He was a great man. Let me show you something, Robbie."

Red Hawk took Robbie for a short visit to the Cadet Chapel at West Point, New York in 1841.

"That is Captain Casey," Red Hawk said as his eyes trained on the only person in the Chapel, sitting on the end of a pew beneath a wooden slatted window. The shards of light coming through the window bathed Casey's face with alternating light and darkness. Casey had made the pilgrimage to his alma mater in search of relief for his nagging conscience.

The boys sat near Casey. Robbie could not help but notice the many bronze plaques and cannon commemorating the conquests— and losses—of the Academy's graduates mounted upon each of the walls. Cannon, the boy pondered, in a chapel? Robbie continued to survey the beautiful simplicity of the Chapel: white walls, white benches covered with crimson seat cushions, four Greek-style pillars on either side of the center aisle.

Casey stirred in his seat, drawing a thump of the boy's heart. Robbie saw the stick in Casey's hands. The officer was thinking of Red Hawk as he carved away on the shaft with a small knife. Robbie followed Casey's eyes to the magnificent "Peace and War" mural above the altar. The captain studied the scene depicted in the mural, a woman in a flowing white dress, a man holding the American flag, and, centered between them, the nation's symbol, the bald eagle with its wings outstretched and holding a streamer in its beak with the motto E Pluribus Unum. The stars strewn above the heads of the figures proclaimed the majesty of the heavens.

Casey mocked the Biblical passage framed below the eagle in the mural: Righteousness exalteth a nation: But sin is a reproach to any people. Prov. XIV.

"Righteousness? What we did to those innocent people was not 'righteousness.' I thought this school was about protecting people's freedoms. We stripped freedoms away from them! Is that not a 'sin?' Well?..."

Casey paused, inviting a response to his questions from God. Receiving none, he continued his soliloquy, "How many people did we kill for no reason? How many people died from exposure or disease? At least Red Hawk and Sunflower survived." His voice began to rise slightly, "But how many died?"

Again he paused, soliciting a Divine response.

Casey waited quietly, chipping away on the shaft. Robbie's heart leapt with excitement when he recognized the pillars of the Chapel taking form on the stick.

For over an hour Casey sat brokenhearted, occasionally wiping moisture from his eyes, still waiting and hoping for a reply. The captain then rose slowly from his pew, looked to the cross sitting upon the altar and made one last plea, "I need some help on this." He lingered once more—to no avail, and shuffled out.

"He resigned his commission not long after this, Robbie, and returned to his farm in Alabama," Red Hawk offered with little emotion.

Robbie awoke with a completely different outlook on his life and later that night commended the story to his journal.

# The Trail Where They Wept

*The whole scene since I have been in this country has been nothing but a heartrending one, and such a one as I would be glad to get rid of as soon as the circumstances will permit.*
—General John Wool, Commanding Officer,
US Army Forces in Charge of Cherokee Removal,
To the Honorable Lewis Cass, Secretary of War
September 10, 1836

Robbie was so appalled by the events of the previous night's visit that he decided to research the Trail of Tears in earnest. He began with his history teacher that morning.

"Good morning, Robbie," welcomed Ms. Hastings, a warm, engaging 27-year-old fifth-year teacher.

"Good morning," Robbie replied somewhat drearily.

Ms. Hastings immediately picked up on Robbie's unusual demeanor.

"Is everything O.K., Robbie?"

"Yes. Well, maybe. Do you know anything about the Trail of Tears—the Cherokee removal?"

A surprised Ms. Hastings replied, "I've read a fair amount about that event, Robbie. Why do you ask?"

"Well, I found out about some of it recently and I really hadn't known anything about it, that's all. I'm just curious."

"We don't really cover it in this course, but I'd be glad to share what I can with you."

Just before the bell Robbie's classmates filed in. As the

bell sounded to begin class, Ms. Hastings asked Robbie, "Why don't you come by on your free period and we'll talk about it?"

"O.K., but I don't want to bother you with it."

"No problem—just come by and let's see what we can cover."

In preparation for Robbie's questions, Ms. Hastings pulled a couple of her references. She had studied the Trail of Tears during her undergraduate work, and she located the topic in her well-organized and labeled notebooks. She scanned them quickly. Her bookshelf was full of dozens and dozens of history books. When Robbie arrived, Ms. Hastings could still see the boy's anguish.

"Would you like to share with me why this topic has suddenly become so important, Robbie?"

"I'd rather not, but I would like to hear what you think about it."

"How much do you know?"

"Not much. I know that it was the forced removal of the Cherokee Nation to the west. And it happened around 1838 and 1839. That's really it."

Ms. Hastings was concerned about Robbie's sudden interest, but began, "O.K., well, the Trail of Tears, as it has come to be known by most historians, or more correctly, 'The Trail Where They Wept,' was a rather dark chapter in the history of the United States. While there have certainly been a number of others, many people feel this is among the very worst.

"This is a pretty long and complicated story, Robbie. But the key items, I think, are relatively simple to understand. The core issue was that the American settlers wanted the Cherokee land. Our history is obviously full of such encroachments, beginning with Columbus, and then the Plymouth Colony, through the Cherokee, the wars on the Great Plains, and culminating, for all practical purposes, with the Battle at Wounded Knee. These tensions have always been a part of humankind, and they have certainly been prevalent in the history of the Americas.

"Remember that the Louisiana Purchase was executed in 1803 and the Corps of Discovery—the Lewis and Clark Expedition—mapped out what the country had actually bought, returning in 1806. There was enormous interest in the West. And so, over a period of time, the westward push of the white settlers was bound to create more and more problems. In order to ease both existing and future frictions, the United States government began to arrange a series of treaties with the Cherokee which, on the surface, were to benefit both sides. In exchange for land cessions the government paid the natives certain monetary amounts. Of course, we have seen that these transactions were very manipulative and over the long term sure to go in the favor of the government. The lands of the Cherokee—and the Creeks, Choctaws, and others— kept shrinking and shrinking.

"As you can imagine, these land cessions caused strife among the leaders of the tribes. Some of the old guard were insistent that they not surrender any lands under any circumstances. The more pragmatic leaders realized that the white settlers were going to come anyway, so they attempted to get some concessions in return. They also hoped that a more clearly defined territory in which the whites could migrate would benefit both sides. But as quickly as they were drawn the new territorial lines were violated by the whites. And so factions began to splinter off among the groups of native leaders, each claiming to represent the interests of the entire nation. Then, of course, the U.S. government would negotiate with the group that offered the least resistance. It's not really hard to understand. I guess it's just human nature. How are you doing so far, Robbie?"

Despite his outward disposition, Robbie replied softly, "Fine."

"Most conventional history books don't treat the Indian

Wars with the rigor and objectivity the subject merits—at least in my opinion. In addition to the actual conflicts, skirmishes, battles, and wars with the Indians, the presence of the whites caused them to suffer in many other ways. I've already mentioned the bogus treaties. But most people don't realize how badly the diseases brought by the Europeans ravaged the natives. Hundreds of thousands of natives died from smallpox alone.

"I think the other aspect so difficult to follow and understand was the nature of the alliances formed among the settlers, different countries, the United States government, and various tribes. These alliances frequently shifted or changed altogether, often pitting former allies against each other.

"One particular example is relevant to this painful story. You see, before Andrew Jackson became president he was a famous army general who made his name by—you guessed it—fighting Indians. One battle in particular was at Horseshoe Bend, on the Tallapoosa River in Alabama, on March 27, 1814. Jackson's mission was to defeat the Creeks there. Well, in order to gain as much advantage on the Creeks as possible, Jackson enlisted the services of about 500 Cherokee—about one-quarter of his total force."

Robbie was amazed to hear this fact.

"And so they defeated the Creek—actually they massacred them—and Jackson became a hero. There were several accounts of the battle that suggest Jackson was saved at least once by a Cherokee warrior and that due to their battle assignments the Cherokee losses were in disproportion to those of the white soldiers.

"One of the reasons this removal is so tragic is that many of the Cherokee who assisted Jackson felt that he would not betray the loyalty they had rendered to him. The warriors who fought for Jackson as young men were now tribal elders and leaders. They were convinced that Jackson would not have won that battle—or perhaps even survived—without their participation and so, as president, he would return the favor by not signing their eviction order. There was no way he could turn his back on them—but they were wrong.

"Over many years negotiations took place between the government and various delegations of Cherokee. Finally, a faction calling themselves the New Echota group signed away all of the Cherokee lands to the United States and agreed to be resettled in Indian Territory west of the Mississippi River in what is now Arkansas and Oklahoma.

"That decision did not go over well back in Cherokee Territory. Another group was immediately dispatched to Washington to lobby against the validity of the treaty, arguing that the group that signed the agreement did not represent the true will of the people and were acting for themselves. All efforts failed however, and a short time later the army began rounding up Indians for removal. Up to the last minute, the Cherokee were sure that they would not—and *could* not—be forced to leave.

"Finally, soldiers began appearing at farms to round up natives to be sent to temporary holding pens for further disposition to the West. Some escaped to the hills and later re-formed into what is now called the 'Eastern Band' of the Cherokee. The group that eventually went west became known as the 'Western Band.' When the groups all finally arrived in Indian Territory, there were tremendous difficulties and a few assassinations of the leaders who had sold the lands. It's a very tragic story, Robbie.

"Many historians believe that about 4,000 of the original population of about 16,000 died during the removal, most due to sickness along the Trail or in the holding pens.

"Sickness?" Robbie interrupted.

"Sickness. Whooping cough, cholera, exposure. The holding pens bred virulent diseases, particularly cholera. When the groups finally moved out, the soldiers prodded the natives along like cattle and just kept marching them west. It didn't matter if they were sick. Besides, most of the groups of a thousand-or-so had only one doctor assigned. They had very little clothing, blankets, food, or water. Many times dead bodies were simply left along the roadside. The commanding officer, General Winfield Scott, ordered his soldiers to treat the natives with as much dignity and respect as possible, but I think history has shown that the vast majority of the natives were poorly treated and, in many cases, taken advantage of.

"I have a few books here if you would like to read more about this. The first one is called *Take the Cannoli*, written by Sarah Vowell, a social commentator on National Public Radio. The book contains a collection of essays. The one you want is entitled 'What I See When I Look at the Face on the $20 Bill.' I've tagged it for you. That one is good for an overview. The other book is called *Trail of Tears* by John Ehle. This one is much more historical. You can get all of the names, dates, places, historical documentation, and details of the whole story. It's also very good.

"Let me just point out two passages that I marked when I read this book. Perhaps these observations will provide you with some sense of what was actually happening at the time. The first is a letter from the famous poet Ralph Waldo Emerson to then-President Martin Van Buren expressing his dismay over the entire affair:

A crime is projected that confounds our under-standings by its magnitude. A crime that really deprives us as well as the Cherokee of a country. For how could we call the conspiracy that should crush these poor Indians our government, or the land that was cursed by their parting and dying imprecations our country any more? You, sir, will bring down the renowned chair in which you sit into infamy if your

seal is set to this instrument of perfidy. And the name
of this nation, hitherto the sweet omen of religion
and liberty, will stink to the world.

Robbie sat quietly as he absorbed Emerson's comments.

"The other is the actual proclamation from General Scott,
announcing the removal and advising the Cherokee to coop-
erate. When you get a chance take a look at the language used
in this, Robbie." The boy scanned the document.

"I think that covers the frame, Robbie, but there's certainly
much more to this story. Has that been enough for now?"

"Yes. More than enough. Thanks very much, Ms. Hastings."

"Are you sure you don't want to tell me why this is so
important to you?"

"I'm fine. It's just a personal thing."

"O.K. Well, just let me know if you need some help. You
don't seem quite yourself today."

"It's O.K., Ms. Hastings. Don't worry about me. Thanks
for the information and the books. I'll take a look at them."

Upon his return from school, Robbie stared at the stick for
quite a while and then sat down to study Ms. Hastings' books.

# The Spirit in the Stick

*I count him braver who overcomes his desires than him who conquers his
enemies; for the hardest victory is over self.*
— Aristotle

Having finally deduced the timing of the cycle, at the next
full moon Robbie was expecting Red Hawk's visit.

*"Hi, Red Hawk. I was hoping to see you tonight."*

*"Really? Why tonight?"*

*"Well, I think I figured out when you've been visiting me. Is it
during the full moon of each month?"*

*"Yes, it is. I'm glad you were able to calculate the timing. What
would you like to learn tonight?"*

*"Well, you seem to have shown me about all of the custodians,
and you mentioned that your grandfather gave you the stick. Was
he the only other custodian? Were there others? Where did he get
it?"*

*"Well, I guess this is as good a time as any to share with you
the story of my grandfather. He didn't share this story with me
until he was about to die.*

*"You've noticed that this stick of yours is really an Iroquois
stick. And you also know quite well by now that my grandfather
was a Cherokee."*

Robbie nodded that he understood.

*"Well, the story wasn't quite that simple. For generations before
the birth of my grandfather, the Cherokee and Iroquois intermit-*

*tently raided each other's villages, killing, robbing, and kidnapping. No one is quite sure how long this went on or which side could claim more success. It's certain, though, that these skirmishes went on for many generations and with great loss and misery to both sides. Since both of our tribes share many similarities in language, it is probable that ages ago we were from the same people. For some reason, perhaps just natural migration of small factions, the tribes gradually became two distinct groups and found themselves fighting just as any other rival tribes might."*

*Robbie listened intently.*

*"When my grandfather was just an infant, his father was murdered in one of those raids, and he was abducted by the Iroquois. When he was brought back to the Iroquois homeland, he was given to a man whose wife and son had been killed not two years before in a similar raid initiated by the Cherokee. The man's name was Rising Sun, and he had been a powerful and highly respected warrior in his clan. In the attack he was badly injured and left for dead. When he finally regained consciousness and realized he had allowed his wife and son to be killed, he fell into a severe depression.*

*"When the Iroquois raiding party returned with the young boy, Running Water, who became my grandfather, Rising Sun took him in as his own son. Over some period of time Rising Sun broke free of his melancholy and, though never completely recovering from his loss, began to consider the captured boy his Iroquois son. All the while the boy's adopted grandfather treated the boy in like fashion, loving and teaching him like his own grandson.*

*"Running Water never knew of his true birth. When he was very young, he recalled that he questioned his father two or three times concerning the loss of his mother. In each case, Rising Sun responded truthfully enough, at least in regard to his wife: 'She was killed in a raid by the Cave People.' Then, Running Water told me, his father would weep silently for several minutes, unable to discuss the situation any further. At his young age Running Water did not know the shame that Rising Sun carried with him, not to mention the actual loss of the two most important people in*

*his life. After questioning a few times and receiving the same dreary reply, Running Water stopped asking the question, to spare his father more pain and tears."*

Robbie continued to absorb every word.

*"It was not until Running Water was about fourteen years of age that a mean-spirited relative mentioned to him the true origin of his birth. Running Water felt a wave of nausea pass through his body, and he vomited violently and writhed on the ground. He felt as though his whole life, his whole identity, had been stripped from him.*

*"'This can't be true! My father has loved me my whole life. How could I be of another tribe?' Running Water screamed to himself.*

*"When he gathered enough strength to get back to his feet, he returned to his home and asked his father if this story was true. His father admitted that it was and shared what information he could with Running Water.*

*"'It is true, my son. You are one of the Cave People. What I have been telling you all these years about my wife, though I regret she is not your mother, has been true. She was killed along with our only son when the marauders from the south attacked us twelve years ago.*

*"'A short time later a skirmish party from our tribe arranged a retaliatory attack. I was unable to participate because I was still recovering from my severe wounds. When the party returned, they presented you to me to replace my son. From the beginning I treated you like my own blood. Ever since, you have been everything that a father could ask for in a son. For keeping your true birth from you for my own selfish reasons I will be forever scorned by the Great Spirit.'"*

Red Hawk continued, *"My grandfather, though feeling like his heart had been shattered, understood some of his father's motives and was beginning to try to find a way to forgive him. As a boy of fourteen, Running Water was well aware of the skirmishes that had occurred between the Iroquois and the Cherokee, several other peripheral tribes, and the encroaching white settlers. His greatest confusion was the nature of his father's love. Over the years he had loved Running Water so completely that he suddenly began to marvel that Rising Sun was capable of such true affection in the wake of such a loss. My grandfather also thought long and hard about the role of his own people in this matter. Neither side seemed completely in the right.*

*"After a few weeks of soul-searching, Running Water knew deep in his heart that he must return to his people and asked Rising Sun if he might consider letting him go. Rising Sun told him, 'I have already deprived you of your childhood, my son. I will suffer the wrath of the Great Spirit for having done so. How can I keep you here one minute longer? You must return to your people. With tomorrow's sun you will embark on your journey. Let us prepare.'*

*"Rising Sun had no doubt that all he had taught his adopted son would serve him well in his trek. He was a strong, resourceful young man. And so, the next morning, the boy left his village with a single bag over his shoulder. His father bade the boy good-bye. Rising Sun wept for days, having suffered the curse of losing a second son."*

*Robbie continued to listen silently.*

*"A few days later, Running Water wandered into a village of his people. He identified himself and asked for his family. The woman he said this to jumped for joy and immediately called for Beautiful Way.*

*"Beautiful Way came running in response to the scream. 'This is Running Water. He has returned from the dead!' said the woman. Running Water's mother fell to her knees and stared at him from head to toe. She slowly stood and stared deeply into his eyes, confirming the boy as her long-dead son. She wailed in joy, fell again, and hugged his knees.*

*"When his mother held him Running Water felt an incredible wave of love—and confusion. It took Running Water some time to integrate into his tribe. Later he married a woman of the Bear Clan."*

*Robbie hadn't suspected any of this history, for Red Hawk had not hinted at such an incredible and improbable childhood for Running Water.*

*"So," Red Hawk continued, "Now to the stick."*

*Robbie had completely forgotten about his original question.*

*Red Hawk took Robbie to see for himself. An old Iroquois chief was sitting on a tree stump, plying a hickory branch.*

*"Who's that?" Robbie whispered.*

*"That's my grandfather's adopted grandfather, Mountain Snow. He's carving the stick that you have right now."*

*Robbie stared in awe. A tingling feeling much stronger even than the one he had felt when Captain Lewis initially handed him the stick shot through his body, causing him to become light-headed.*

*The Indian boy pointed a few yards to the right, and Robbie saw the stick hanging from a stand constructed of five large branches, two on each end tied to form a large "V" on the bottom and a small "V" at the top, supporting the other, longer, stick laid perpendicularly between them. The stick was draped over one side with another branch slipped through its webbing to hold its position on the rack.*

*Robbie asked if they could go and look at the stick on the rack and Red Hawk immediately led him there.*

*"This is the one which has been passed down through my sister's descendants. That one," Red Hawk turned his eyes to his great-great-grandfather's hands, "is the one I presented to Lieutenant Casey and has been passed down to you."*

*Red Hawk and Robbie stood and watched the old man as he worked tirelessly and meticulously on making the pair of sticks perfect. Nothing less would do for his eight-year-old grandson. The old man spent several hours carving a scene of a woman with arms extended on one shaft and a baby with arms reaching back to his mother on the other.*

*"My grandfather received these sticks a few weeks after this, on his eighth birthday. He asked his grandfather about the carvings. Mountain Snow simply said that the picture was of his daughter reaching for her son during the raid in which she was killed."*

*Robbie was shaken to realize the gruesome meaning of the unknown carving on his stick.*

*"When I received the sticks, they meant a great deal to me. For any young man in our tribe, these sticks symbolized the first steps toward manhood. My grandfather presented these sticks to me on my eighth birthday as well. As soon as I touched the sticks I could immediately feel the power and spirit of the warrior in my great-great-grandfather and my grandfather. When I was a boy stickball was a critical part of my life in each of my tribes. It was a way for us to be accepted as men into our tribe. When we were still too young to go into battle with our older brothers and fathers, it substituted as a means to show our strength, skill, and courage, the same traits that would make us successful in defense of our tribe. When we became older, we still played with incredible passion, mostly to invite the favor of our gods, to strengthen our boys, to earn respect for our clans in contests with others, and to continue to parade our physical courage."*

*"Did your grandfather say anything to you when he gave you the sticks?"*

*"We talked for a while when he presented the sticks to me. He carved the picture of the hawk—for my name—on the shaft while we talked. He explained that the game would teach me valuable lessons in preparation for manhood. He said above all things that I must be prepared to defend the tribe, that I must develop the skills, strength, and courage to do so. He then said, and I remember this exactly, 'You must first master yourself...before you can lead others.' In fact, he carved that saying onto my sticks, half on one, half on the other. I remember him telling me that when his grandfather gave him the sticks that he was a bit surprised to be given two. Most boys were given only one. Looking back later he said that his grandfather probably gave him two because he was a member of two tribes and because the Cherokee played with two sticks. His grandfather obviously didn't tell him those reasons at the time, but he certainly was mindful of the situation and crafted them accordingly. But beyond what he said to me that day, he*

*passed his spirit to me through the stick. I learned more every day. I could always feel my grandfather's spirit in the stick."*

*Robbie remembered the writing around the head of the stick. "So that is what it says on the top of my—I mean your—stick?"*

*"Yes, and it is your stick. It was written by my grandfather in our native Cherokee language. A few years earlier a man of our tribe named Sequoia had devised our writing system, the first such system among Native Americans. My grandfather immediately sought to learn the writing and teach it to me. The stick that you have has the first part of the saying. It says 'You must first master yourself.' The other part of the saying, 'before you can lead others,' is completed on the other stick, and my sister has passed that down to her descendants."*

*Robbie could hardly believe all of this and was suddenly intrigued by the notion that the other stick might be in the hands of someone else who might be benefiting from it as he was.*

*Red Hawk told Robbie that he would come visit him again and bade farewell.*

"Red Hawk showed me an unbelievable story. There's another stick!" Robbie proudly proclaimed to his parents in the morning.

"Really? How is that?" asked his mother.

"There were originally two—which Red Hawk got as a set. You know the writing on mine? It's only part of a saying that is finished on the other stick! It says, 'You must first master yourself' Red Hawk said that the other one was passed down through his sister. It says, 'before you can lead others.'"

"That's a great saying. It would be pretty amazing if we could find out about the other one," said his dad.

Robbie headed off to school with yet another new wave of energy.

John and Mary Jones looked at each other in disbelief once again. "This whole thing is really incredible, Mary. I'm still having a hard time believing that all of this is possible and that we're involved in it. How did it happen to us?"

# We Admired You, We Respected You, and We Loved You

*I never return to this place without my heart thumping with a sense of history. I sense the great warriors that have gone before us behind every tree and pillar and feel a renewed obligation to be worthy of their company.*
—Vice Admiral James Bond Stockdale
U.S. Naval Academy Class of '47
Former Prisoner of War

Lewis arrived an hour early for his meeting with Robbie and his family at Navy-Marine Corps Memorial Stadium. The time allowed him to walk the stadium at his own pace. He was well beyond the need to relive his glory days on that field. He was more interested now in the stadium itself, the names of the battles emblazoned on the facades, the many plaques citing memorials to fallen shipmates and classmates, and the dedication plaque itself:

DEDICATION
THIS STADIUM IS DEDICATED TO THOSE
WHO HAVE SERVED AND WILL SERVE AS
UPHOLDERS OF THE TRADITIONS AND
RENOWN OF THE NAVY AND MARINE CORPS
OF THE UNITED STATES. MAY IT BE A PERPET-
UAL REMINDER THAT THE NAVY AND MARINE

CORPS ARE ORGANIZATIONS OF MEN
TRAINED TO LIVE NOBLY AND SERVE COURA-
GEOUSLY: IN PEACE, CHAMPIONS OF OUR
INTEGRITY: IN WAR, DEFENDERS OF OUR
FREEDOM.

As he walked, Lewis pondered the hundreds of athletes who had competed on that field and the many that had been lost in combat. Few days went by when he didn't think of his fallen comrades.

Robbie and his family arrived at 1:15.

"Well, are we all ready?" Lewis asked.

"We can't wait," replied Mrs. Jones.

"O.K. I know that in the last few months all of you, especially Robbie, have learned a great deal about the history of the game. I thought it would be good to get in touch with the Army-Navy game itself. Tonight is the 76th meeting in the storied rivalry. There is simply no bigger game for either of these two teams. It is going to be a treat, I'm sure. But before the game, I'd like to take you on a special tour. I'll explain as we go."

"Sounds great," agreed John Jones.

"Since we're already here, why don't we start with the stadium?" Lewis proposed rhetorically. "Some people have called this facility a memorial that doubles as a stadium. I like to think of it that way myself. There are over 400 plaques placed all around this stadium and about 8,000 seats offered as tributes to people or military units. And you can see the battles commemorated on the facades." He walked the family around the same loop he had just completed, offering details of the key points, the names of and a few facts about the battles.

"Would you mind taking a short ride?" Lewis asked the family.

"Not at all. Please," said Mrs. Jones.

They drove from the stadium through downtown Annapolis onto the grounds of the academy and to the Lacrosse Office in MacDonough Hall. Coach Richie Meade was expecting their arrival.

"Coach, thanks for having us. Let me introduce Robbie, his sister Catherine, and their parents, John and Mary Jones."

Coach Meade then introduced the family to his staff and a long-time supporter of the program, the *Grand Dame* of Navy Lacrosse, M.G. Buchanan who had happened by to wish the coach good luck. "It's great having you all here. Our players are very excited about the game tonight. I hope you are, too. I understand that Captain Lewis is going to escort you on a special tour this afternoon. I wish I could go with you, but we still need to finalize some things for the game. Where are you going?"

Lewis cut in on the answer, "I'm going to surprise them."

"Well, I'm sure you know how important Captain Lewis has been to the Naval Academy and to Navy Lacrosse."

Coach Meade pulled a framed magazine article off his wall and handed it to Robbie. It was an autographed picture of Lewis from a 1966 copy of the *Baltimore Sun Magazine*. The article was entitled, "The Greatest Lacrosse Man Ever." Coach Meade pointed out some of the other pictures on his wall. He was extremely proud of the program and took every opportunity to share his pride.

"These are our three players who have played for the United States team. He pointed to Jeff Long, Class of '77, Glen Miles, '86, and Andy Ross, '97. We are very proud of all of them. While members of the USA team, each won the World Championship. I think each of these guys would tell you how great it was to play for Navy. But to have the additional honor of playing for their country was something they'll never forget." The coach pointed to another picture of two of his players from the Class of 2000 at the Graduation Week Prizes and Awards Ceremony.

"This is also one of my favorite pictures, Robbie. These two young men had outstanding careers here at Navy, but it wasn't easy for either of them. This is Jon Brianas, who had to battle through cancer while he was here. He received the Vice Admiral Edward C. Waller Lacrosse Award, given annually to the 'midshipman who has contributed most to the spirit, morale, and well-being of the lacrosse team.' And this is Mickey Jarboe holding the Naval Academy Athletic Association Sword, awarded to 'the most outstanding athlete of his class.' Mickey's story is amazing also—since he didn't even start for his high school team. When he graduated from here, he had been selected as the outstanding goalie in the country twice! These guys are what Navy Lacrosse is all about. We are very proud of them. I hope you'll see what I mean tonight."

Coach Meade shared more history with the family, citing seventeen National Championships, 331 All-Americas, and several Hall-of-Fame players and coaches during the program's ninety years. Lewis thanked Coach Meade for the visit. Meade presented Robbie and Catherine copies of the team's program and a ball autographed by all of his players and Lewis.

From MacDonough Hall the group took a short walk to Lejeune Hall, home of Navy's Olympic-sized swimming pool as well as the Navy Athletic Hall-of-Fame. Lewis walked his guests slowly past an assortment of memorabilia, including a football from the 1963 Cotton Bowl.

Lewis grudgingly obliged a request to point out items that honored him, so he waved at a couple of pictures, then the huge plaque recording the recipients of the Naval Academy Athletic Association Sword. Lewis's name was listed in the Class of '66, immediately below Heisman Trophy winner and NFL Hall-of-Famer Roger Staubach for the Class of '65, Tom Lynch '64, who had recently completed a tour as Superintendent, and the late Donald C. McLaughlin '63, who had been a "firstie" (senior) when Lewis was a plebe, and who had died in Vietnam. The recipient for the Class of '61 was Navy's other Heisman Trophy recipient, Joe Bellino. Understanding the stature of Bellino and Staubach Mr. Jones was the most impressed of the group. The family scanned the plaque beginning with the honoree of 1893, C.S. Bookwater of football and crew, all the way to the Class of 2000, Mickey Jarboe.

Lewis hurried the group past his Hall-of-Fame plaque. This visit wasn't about him. The true purpose was to show his guests the plaque dedicated to his late coach:

WILLIS P. (Bildy) BILDERBACK
NAVY LACROSSE COACH
1959-1972
Record 117-18-1
NINE NATIONAL CHAMPIONSHIPS 1960-67, 70
EIGHT CONSECUTIVE (1960-1967)
FIVE UNDEFEATED SEASONS 1960, 62, 64, 65, 66
92 ALL-AMERICAS
LACROSSE COACH OF THE YEAR 1960
MEMBER LACROSSE HALL OF FAME
BILDY SAID, "THE GREATEST EXPERIENCE OF MY
LIFE HAS BEEN COACHING MIDSHIPMEN."
BILDY, WE ARE THE FORTUNATE ONES. WE CAN'T
THANK YOU ENOUGH FOR BEING OUR COACH
AND FRIEND. YOU WERE AN EXCEPTIONAL
TACTICIAN, TEACHER, AND MOTIVATOR. YOU
GAVE US SO MUCH AND INSTILLED IN US A
SPECIAL LOVE FOR THE GAME. YOU MADE US
WINNERS ON THE FIELD AND IN LIFE, AND MADE
US DIG DEEP WITHIN OURSELVES TO DO OUR
BEST. WE ADMIRED YOU, WE RESPECTED YOU
AND WE LOVED YOU.
THE TEAM
DONATED BY THE NAVAL ACADEMY ATHLETIC
ASSOCIATION

Lewis allowed the family to read the inscription on the plaque. "He was a great coach. I think at the time we all knew it—but it means so much more to us now."

Next Lewis drove the family to the State of Maryland World War II Memorial located just across the Severn River from the Yard. Upon arriving at the Memorial, Lewis allowed the family a few minutes to peruse the magnificent circular formation of granite and marble. The flags of Maryland and the United States hung heavily from their supports, about thirty feet above the central icon. The Memorial was offered as a tribute to the natives of Maryland who lost their lives while serving in the United States Army, Navy, Marine Corps, Coast Guard, and Army Air Corps of World War II.

Lewis stood in front of the inscription of Jack Turnbull's name carved into the black granite. In the polished rock he could see his own reflection. Lewis stared at his image superimposed on Jack's name and pondered what his life would have been like without the stick. It was too daunting a thought to elicit a coherent response. Lewis almost unconsciously began tracing the inscription of Jack's name. His guests slowly gathered and simply stared at the name. No words were necessary.

The next stop was in nearby Davidsonville and All Hallows' Episcopal Church. Lewis drove past the sign announcing the establishment of the church in 1692 and proceeded up a slight incline on a gravel road. They were greeted by a timid and solitary rabbit who ambled away as they opened the car doors. All of them saw the cemetery located adjacent to and behind the beautiful old brick building. Lewis walked the family around the side of the church to the graveyard.

"This is where Jack Turnbull and his parents are buried," Lewis said respectfully. He escorted the group to the general area and allowed them to review the stones without further comment, letting the tranquility of the yard to say what needed to be said. Occasional birds added their voices to the gathering.

As Robbie scanned the graveyard, his eyes were captured by many large, ornate stones. He automatically surveyed those, the stones having achieved their purpose of gathering attention, but he scanned the names to no avail. Then he noticed a small American flag hanging limply on its stick, placed next to a gravestone. It was a rather nondescript, baseless stone, about two feet high, with a cross inscribed above the name. The stone was grayed by time and partially covered with moss on the top. He read the inscription:

JOHN
IGLEHART
TURNBULL
MARYLAND
LIEUTENANT COLONEL AIR CORPS
WORLD WAR II
JUNE 30, 1910
OCTOBER 18, 1944

Robbie felt a chill as he realized that the body of Jack Turnbull was located only several feet below his own. He gently stepped back not to offend the great pilot. His family had seen Robbie freeze in his tracks and, taking the cue, joined him.

"A group of veterans comes by on several occasions a year and places these flags on the graves of our countrymen lost in battle." Lewis offered just above a whisper. They looked around the rest of the cemetery and noticed only a few other flags among hundreds of other stones.

They also saw the markers of Jack's grandparents adjacent to his and then the dual stone of his parents just beyond those. Robbie immediately connected with "Mum" as he studied her stone:

TURNBULL

DOUGLAS CLAYLAND     ELIZABETH B. IGLEHART

JULY 23, 1874            APRIL 12, 1875

MARCH 1, 1941         JULY 13, 1957

THEIR FAITH, THEIR STRENGTH

The boy's mind rewound to the scene Red Hawk had provided when Mum received the news of Jack's death and then the scene of her presenting the first Turnbull Award to Stewart McLean.

After allowing another fifteen or twenty minutes for the family to take in the sights and sounds of the cemetery, Lewis quietly led his group back to the car for the continuation of the day. Lewis drove his guests back to Annapolis for an early dinner at the Wharf and fielded more questions as they ate.

"I'd like to get to the game a little early if we can. There is someone I'd like you to meet."

Again, Lewis hit his target time exactly and found Tommy Adams at a pre-game reception in his honor at the stadium pavilion. Upon sighting Lewis, Tommy broke off his conversation and came to greet him. The old friends embraced. "Thanks for coming, Jim."

"Glad I could make it. Let me introduce you to some special guests. This is Robbie and his family. John, Mary, and Catherine Jones."

Tommy and his wife Joyce greeted them warmly and asked how they knew Captain Lewis.

Lewis said simply, "We've become friends over the last few months through, let's just say, a mutual friend named Red Hawk."

Tommy's face beamed, and he smiled at Lewis. He knew. He knew that Robbie was now the custodian of the special stick. Tommy thought it would be useful for Robbie to hear the unique circumstances of how Captain Lewis would select his sticks during the years he played at Navy.

"Robbie, do you know how good Captain Lewis was when he was here? Well, when our yearly shipments of five hundred sticks came in, Coach Bilderback instructed me to call Jim first and have him select ten sticks for the upcoming season. *Then* I would call the seniors. I don't think the others guys knew that Jim got first crack. I suppose that even if they did, they didn't mind much. Jim would spend hours looking for a stick that matched his special stick—the one Mr. Turnbull had given him. He never was able to find one quite like it, but he picked out the ten best. The deal I struck with Jim for letting him choose first was that as he pondered his selections, he would let me study his special stick. I became intimately attuned to the marvelous balance and harmony of the wood, gut, and leather. For decades I always used the characteristics of that stick as the basis for how I strung and balanced Navy lacrosse sticks. It was the seed from which all of the other sticks grew. None of the other guys knew about that, either—or even Coach Bilderback—just Jim and I."

"Robbie," Lewis said, "Tommy is being honored at half-time tonight for his service to the Naval Academy. You see, he has been the lacrosse team's equipment manager for forty years. Tommy is the single greatest expert on lacrosse sticks in the world today. We call him the Stick Doctor. Many of the innovations that have come about over the years in regard to equipment improvement began with Tommy. I can't tell you how much he's meant to me personally when I was playing and to the hundreds of other midshipmen over the years."

It was an uncommonly warm evening in Annapolis as play began. Lewis let the play speak for itself. Robbie was struck by the pace, intensity, and physicality of the game. Each ground ball, each one-on-one, was hotly contested.

Navy took a 7-3 lead into half-time.

Shortly after the teams went to their locker rooms, Director of Athletics Jack Lengyel presided over a group heading to the center of the field. With Lengyel were Mike Gottleib '70, Carl Tamulevich '68, currently Assistant Director of Athletics and a National Lacrosse Hall-of-Famer, and Tommy.

A public address announcer regaled the crowd of over 6,000 with Tommy's many achievements during his forty years. After the remarks, the announcer then directed attention to Mike Gottleib, general manager of the "Navy Old Goats"—a team of former Navy players who compete annually in the Vail Shootout—and graphic designer to present Tommy with an original watercolor depicting his tenure. Tommy's face graced the main body of the work, and in each corner stood vignettes of key points; Jim Lewis, the Old Goats, Willis Bilderback, and Jeff Long.

Navy played another solid half, earning a 10-4 victory and their fourth straight win over Army, a remarkable achievement, only performed a handful of times in the history of the 80-year rivalry. All-America Adam Borcz scored four goals that night, ending his career as the all-time leading scorer among Navy midfielders.

"Robbie, you know when we talk about getting on the wall and working on your skills? I sat quietly in the bleachers last night and watched Adam take 100 shots with both hands after practice before he left. Coach Meade tells me that he does it all the time. Also with all of the work he's put into lacrosse he's not allowed his grades to slip. He's been selected for the Navy's nuclear power program, which requires strong academic work. It's no surprise that he has achieved what he has. He's a special player."

Lewis brought the family down to the field to congratulate the staff, players, and Tommy, and to meet his former teammate, Carl Tamulevich. Robbie noted the elation on the faces of the Navy players and the utter dejection of their Army counterparts—just like the 1964 game. It hadn't changed much, he thought.

"So, what did you think of the day, Robbie?" Tommy asked.

"Best day of my life," Robbie beamed.

# Rebirth

*Memory grips the past; hope grips the future.*
—Scott Russell Sanders
*Hunting for Hope*

Red Hawk again appeared on the next full moon, the tenth in a row.

*"Hi, Robbie. How have you been doing?"*

*"Great. I went to the Army-Navy game a few days ago. Captain Lewis took my family and me on a tour and then to the game. It was awesome. Navy won!"*

Red Hawk nodded, knowing the story already. *"Did you want to go anywhere specific this time or ask any questions?"*

*"Well, I think we've gotten back to the origin of the stick, haven't we?" Robbie asked.*

*"Yes, we have. There's certainly a lot more to learn about each of the custodians, but perhaps we could just discuss a little bit about where this stick has taken us so far."*

*"Sure."*

Red Hawk began, *"Well, for each of the previous custodians, I've been fortunate to share with them some piece of the story of the stick in the first ten moons. Actually, I attempted to guide them for the most part to the scenes and information I thought would be most useful for their growth as custodian of the stick. It was almost as though they were in a womb for those ten moons, exactly as you and I were in our mothers' wombs, being nourished by their bodies*

155

and the Great Spirit. Then at birth, we were all free to pursue our own forms of knowledge through our own experiences.

"And so it is now for you. I hope that you've grown in this 'womb' of visits. You know the story of the stick. Now it's time to spread your wings, explore on your own, strive to reach your full potential, discover the great mysteries of life, learn the ways of the world, and, perhaps, find your place in it.

"You might recall that the day Captain Lewis presented you with my grandfather's stick, he and your family spared the life of that fledgling which had fallen from a tree."

Robbie's heart warmed when he realized that Red Hawk was familiar with that event and might even have had some hand in it.

Red Hawk continued, "Perhaps it was not a coincidence that for you the first lesson of the stick was one of life. From there you've seen and learned of some of the great tragedies and horrors known to mankind. You've seen death, war, hate, prejudice, injustice. You saw the death of a great hero, Jack Turnbull. And you witnessed his mother, Mum Turnbull, receive the news that her son had died, perhaps the greatest burden that any person must bear.

"You saw the carnage at Gettysburg. You saw the Trail of Tears. You've experienced the cruelty of mankind manifested in those two compelling books, Uncle Tom's Cabin, and Het Achterhuis. But you have also seen acts of honor, mercy, compassion, empathy, and dignity. Remember the heroic dignity of Mrs. Turnbull after Jack's death. You saw the noble actions of Colonel Casey and Colonel Chamberlain at Little Round Top.

"Remember the empathy that Casey showed for the Cherokee, particularly for my sister and me. You saw my great-grandfather release his adopted son to pursue his life with his people. You saw and felt the passion put into the construction of your stick by the Iroquois chief. So many of life's greatest lessons are held in this stick and through the people who have lived noble—yet very ordi-nary—lives.

"In my discussions with each of the custodians over these one-hundred and sixty years, I think that we've all agreed that a great place from which to start our relationship is with the gift of life. And so today, I hope that with this insight into this stick, you might begin your life anew—with a more sensitive appreciation of how truly precious and precarious each of our lives is. From there, I hope that you'll find, like the other custodians, what you want to find in your own life and that you may then find a way to use that insight to help others, much as Lieutenant Casey helped me. You see, beginning with my great-great grandfather and then Casey and the others, this stick has been a tribute to the goodness in people, not the evil.

"Perhaps one of the great lessons in the lives of these men is that to experience the full range of human emotion, one must endure a great array of experiences, both good and bad.

"In order to understand and fully appreciate joy, you must know pain. To know goodness, you must know evil. To know light, you must know darkness. And so it is only through these inextricable opposites, these paradoxes, that we're able to experience the entire spectrum of what life has to offer. There's so much to learn from each of the custodians.

"So now you've seen the past. You're living the present. There are no guarantees for what the future holds. We can only hope. But to know the past and the present is to provide as sound a footing as possible for the trials of the future. I hope the lessons you've learned so far, as well as the many still ahead, will give you a better chance to conquer adversity, master yourself, and make a positive difference in the world.

"I believe this is a stick of life. It is a stick of honor. It is a stick of respect. Above all, though, I think the true spirit of this stick is one of hope.

"The men who have had it before you have made it such. Each of the men was forced to cling to hope while they battled their own frailties, fears, self-doubt, frustration, and disappointments. They learned valuable lessons of leadership and courage in internal and external crucibles. Before they could have an impact on others they were forced to confront themselves. Each has left a legacy of honor, goodness, and leadership to you and me. You will get to add your own signature, your own carving on the stick, to its history as you see fit.

"We both have a great deal more to learn about each other, the custodians of this stick, and the great mysteries of our lives."

With that Red Hawk paused and slowly turned away. Robbie stood silent. On his first step, Red Hawk turned his head back to Robbie and said softly, "My grandfather has always stayed with me when I have needed him. I will stay with you. It is my duty. I owe it not only to him but also to many other people.

"Happy Birthday, Robbie."

Robbie stood briefly confused, thinking that it was not his birth-day. Then as Red Hawk stepped away, he realized that it was.

# The Soul of Nature

*Could a greater miracle take place than for us to look through each other's
eyes for an instant?*
—Henry David Thoreau
*Walden*

Lewis visited Robbie a few days after the tenth moon and
asked the boy if he would mind going for a walk at the park
where they had first met. Robbie eagerly accepted.

As they walked, Lewis began with the usual array of questions concerning school and other general topics, with
predictable replies. Then he posed a few questions to gauge
what insight Robbie had gained from the stick, so that he
might be able to assist him further.

"What do you think the most important thing is that you
have learned from the stick at this point, Robbie?" Lewis
posed.

"I don't think I can really say. I've learned so much. One
thing I can say is that my eyes have been opened to many
things I used to take for granted."

"Like what?"

"Well, just about everything. I've learned so much about
history. I really like *The Story of Mankind* that you gave me.
Before I met you and Red Hawk, history was just a bunch of
boring dates, names, and places in books. Now I realize that
those names were real people with real feelings. I've learned
quite a bit about war.

"I never used to think much about nature, either. I never really looked at the trees, or felt the air or the wind. I do now. The other book you gave me, *Silent Spring*, really helped me understand the balance of nature."

They arrived at a stream and sat down on a log. Lewis allowed the discussion to fade so they could listen to the stream. The boy was quite content to sit and listen to the voice of the water as well. After some ten minutes or so, Robbie finally said softly, "This is one of the things I've learned. I never understood the subtle sounds of nature. It's almost as if the stream can talk. Like it's alive."

Lewis smiled as Robbie continued.

"And the birds, the animals—even the insects. I never noticed any of that."

They listened some more.

"Well, Robbie, I'm glad to hear that. You know these big trees and certainly this little river have been here a lot longer than we have. And they will be here much longer after we leave this world. Since I met Red Hawk all those years ago, I have marveled at the character of rivers, oceans, streams, and lakes. They are the sustainers of life and the roads of commerce. I remember being struck in *Het Achterhuis* by how young Anne had completely acquired sensitivity to nature."

Lewis stood to continue the walk and asked Robbie, "What do you think you've learned about the game?"

"Well, I certainly learned more than I could ever have imagined. It was so cool to see the Cherokee game, and your game against Army, and then this year's Army-Navy game. That ceremony at Hopkins was really amazing.

"Even though I've been playing for a of couple years, I don't think I could have understood the ancient spirit of the game. You and Red Hawk have been a big help with that part. It's helped me with my game. I work a lot harder now than I used to. I think I understand what it means to 'Respect the Game.'"

"What do you think you've learned about yourself?"

Robbie thought for a prolonged period. "I think the biggest thing is the obligation I have to others. I never used to think about that. I mean on my team, at home, at school. I think that's been a constant characteristic of the custodians of the stick. They worked so hard for others. I mean, Red Hawk saved his sister's life and took care of her. And Red Hawk's great-great grandfather gave and taught so much to his adopted grandson. Lieutenant Casey helped the Cherokees. Then Chamberlain could have killed Casey but didn't. He was there for his men despite being shot six times. Jack Turnbull gave his life for others. Doug Turnbull spent his life helping people—including you. And your service to the country and all you have done for me.

"I think the people before me have also been about action. They've done things. I think I've learned a lot about the importance of doing things. The stick has a pretty overwhelming history. I think I'm gonna have to try harder to live up to my part."

Lewis smiled inwardly. He's getting it, he thought. That's pretty amazing for a boy so young. "You are doing great already, Robbie. I'm glad to hear your insights. How far have you gotten on the carvings?"

"I think I've made it through all of the carvings and the inscription."

"Really? What does the writing say?"

"It says, 'You must first master yourself...'"

"Were you able to find out about the rest of the saying?"

"Yes. I guess you know the other stick says, 'before you can lead others.'"

"What do you think the inscription means? The part about mastering yourself."

"I was hoping you might be able to tell me what you think."

"Well, like many of the other issues presented by the stick, it took me a little while to really get in touch with this thought. I think what I've found after all these years is that it's important to be prepared to overcome obstacles. At some point in their lives, most people find that the greatest difficulty they'll face is themselves. They'll get defeated by some external entity—school, work, personal issues—you name it. But the greatest difficulty is usually maintaining the confidence in yourself to move on and use the setback as an opportunity for growth. I suspect it's terribly easy for me to say these things and equally difficult for you to believe them. But it's at those difficult times that you must 'master yourself.' Once you have developed the ability to deal with external—and the subsequent internal—crises, then you'll be in a much better position to positively affect others. It's all about dealing with adversity, I think. What do you think?"

"That sounds good. Thanks."

"What else would you like to discuss?"

"How was it having the stick all those years? Did Red Hawk visit you every month the whole time?"

"Well, as you're already finding out, having the stick for forty-plus years was pretty cool. Just imagine how much you've learned since you got it and multiply it by forty. At all of the critical junctures in my life Red Hawk and Mr. Turnbull were there for me. They helped me a lot.

"And, yes, Red Hawk did visit me every month for the whole time. I know that you've been keeping a journal. Please keep doing that. I started mine after about four months because I didn't realize the dreams were real until then. So I went back and reconstructed the early visits. I think I ended up with over 500 stories in there. I read through it every once in a while."

"Do you think I might be able to look at it sometime?"

"Sure. Remember, I'm here for you just as Mr. Turnbull was for me. My journal has some pretty cool stuff in it. Mr. Turnbull also sent me over a hundred letters. I keep all of it together."

"Do you miss not having the stick?"

"I miss Red Hawk more than I thought I might—but I'm thrilled that you're benefiting from his guidance. Mr. Turnbull shared the very same sentiment with me after a year or so."

They continued the discussion on the way back. When they arrived near their entry point, a soft, warm breeze swept by them. As always Lewis felt it immediately, and Robbie pointed it out a second later. "See, Captain Lewis, I can feel that breeze. Red Hawk has taught me to be sensitive to the wind." Lewis smiled.

Just then a young hawk landed on the brick wall adjacent to the path about thirty yards ahead. The bird looked directly at Robbie and bobbed its head up and down several times. Robbie diverted his path slightly and approached the bird. Lewis stopped and looked on with a great deal of pride as Robbie responded to the silent beckoning of the hawk.

Robbie felt a rush of excitement as the bird communicated with him. The hawk bobbed its head again. Robbie bent over, extended his hand, and allowed the bird to climb on.

Robbie stared carefully into the bird's eyes for some time as it looked straight back. Robbie's gaze took him through the hawk's eyes and into its soul—indeed, into the very soul of Nature. At that instant, Robbie saw and felt his personal and intimate connection with all living things. This connection was far deeper even than his new-found sensitivity to the streams, winds, and trees. This was a living, breathing, moving, thinking organism not terribly unlike himself. What a magnificent creation, he thought.

Robbie considered the miracle of his own life. He made the mental leap to the preposterous notion of the millions of complex processes occurring at exactly the right time and proper sequence within his own body. The chemical balance. His body temperature. His eyes. His organs and muscles. His breathing. His heartbeat. The flow of blood through his veins. For the first time, he became fully conscious of everything within himself. Robbie's life had changed yet again.

After a few minutes of silent exchanges, Robbie offered the hawk the telepathic reply: Our pleasure. He then sent the bird aloft into another soft, warm breeze which had just materialized.

"That was the same bird we met here last year," Robbie proclaimed confidently to Lewis as the bird kited up into the sky.

"How do you know?" asked the captain.

"She thanked us."

# Epilogue

*To live in the hearts and minds of those we leave behind is not to die.*
—United States Naval Academy
*Lucky Bag,* 1983

Long Island National Cemetery July 7, 2002

"O.K., girls, we can go now," I whispered as I began walking softly and slowly to my car. Upon arriving there, I looked down expecting to see my seven-year-old daughter Catherine and my six-year-old niece Olivia on each of my hips, their appointed station all afternoon at a Long Island Ducks minor league baseball game.

I turned, instead, to see Catherine *hugging* the tombstone of my sister Marguerite, her face pressed sideways against the marble, her fingers interlaced on the back side—just able to reach all-the-way around. Olivia was kneeling before the stone of my mother, adjacent to her daughter's, and staring softly at the inscription. The girls sat quietly, occasionally stealing a glance, seeking a cue from each other.

I stood frozen, watching these two girls alternately kneel, sit, and stand before the markers. They switched positions two or three times and exchanged a few quiet words. Catherine was completely engrossed in Marguerite's marker. I watched her pat, caress, and hug the stone. I watched her trace out the letters delicately with her left index finger, as if reading Braille. I tried to identify the expression on her face and in her heart. It was not really sadness, I decided. It looked more like a longing to know this girl who, the marker confirmed, had died before her fifth birthday. A girl she never knew, a girl I never knew. A girl known to me only through a handful of pictures. My sister, yes, but who had died before I was born.

As I watched my daughter clinging to what was left of her deceased aunt and grandmother, my mind was unconsciously overtaken by uncanny parallels to the story of the stick.

I first saw Red Hawk clinging to his mother's body as the soldiers pulled her away.

Then as I considered my mother's gravestone overlooking that of the daughter who predeceased her, my mind's eye saw Mum and Douglas Turnbull's stone standing sentinel over Jack's at All Hallow's.

Next I remembered the lesson Red Hawk had shared with Robbie in regard to the polar opposites of life. How one emotion or experience cannot be reconciled without the other—hope and despair, good and evil, success and failure, pleasure and pain, ignorance and knowledge. My mind added the ultimate and inescapable pair, life and death.

As I continued to study the girls as they puzzled over the stones, I saw Robbie stepping back from Jack Turnbull's grave, pondering the twists of fate that called the great pilot to his premature rest.

My mind then had me consider the range of fortune represented, quite literally, beneath the girls' feet. Below my daughter and niece were a mother who had borne eight children, seven of whom (all boys) continue to live healthy lives, and who herself lived what could only be described as an abundantly fruitful, productive life, and her only daughter, lost at age four after a long illness, never to be known to four of her brothers. Polar opposites yet again.

As I felt Nature in all her glory—the beautiful day, the sun, the grass, the trees, the birds—I thought of the passage

from Anne Frank on the day Jimmy Lewis was born. I rumi-
nated on the majesty, grandeur, and multiplicity of Nature.
I joined in the reverence with which Red Hawk and all Indians
held the Earth—the rhythm of their lives entwined so intimately with the rhythm of the Earth.

What a sight, watching those girls. The lives, the minds,
the hearts, the lessons. The hope that filled me was overwhelming. The flood of thoughts, visions, and emotions
made me realize all I had learned from the story manifested
in the stick and in the lives of its remarkable custodians.

A warm breeze suddenly swept by, shaking me from my
trance. A chill penetrated every part of my body. It was too
remarkable, too eerie, and too *personal* to be a coincidence. It
was Red Hawk. Miraculously I had just become part of the
story myself. My mind raced back through my entire journey
with Jim Lewis and Bruce Turnbull. I stood humbly thinking
I was not worthy of their goodness in sharing their relationship with Red Hawk with me.

I looked up and thanked Red Hawk for bestowing an even
higher honor upon me.

The girls finally came back, and Catherine stunned me
by saying, "I don't want to die, Daddy. But if I do, it'll be O.K.
because I'll get to be with Marguerite and Nana."

I stood silent a few seconds longer, reminding myself once
again that I was the most fortunate father on Earth. I thought
of what I have told Catherine many times: I hope some day
you'll get to love someone as much as Mom and I love you
and your little brother. I added an unspoken addendum to
that wish: I hope you'll live long enough to experience something as sublime as I just had.

Finally, I climbed into my car—shaken yet solidified,
humbled yet uplifted, scared yet secure, overwhelmed yet
eased, emptied yet fulfilled, forever changed yet forever the
same. Rededicated. Rededicated to the game of lacrosse, to
Nature, to all who have helped and supported me along the

way, to my family, friends, and colleagues, to my students, to my wife, and, mostly, to our children.

# Special Thanks

This project would not have been possible if not for the gracious and positive support of many people. First and foremost, CAPT Jim Lewis, USNA '66 who allowed me to use his career as the cornerstone of the story. MAJ R. Bruce Turnbull, USMA '57 was equally gracious in offering information, support, and latitude with the lives of his father, grandmother, and uncle. I was honored that Dr. Thomas Vennum, author of *American Indian Lacrosse: Little Brother of War*—the definitive work on the history of the game—took time to review and improve my work at a critical juncture.

Having the dean of lacrosse coaches, Mr. Bob Scott, offer introductory remarks to this story is one of the great honors that has ever been bestowed upon me. His unflagging support and assistance were crucial at every point in this process.

The kind words provided by Jeff Long, USNA '77 of Ithaca College, Dom Starsia of the University of Virginia, Jack Emmer of the United States Military Academy and the USA team, Richie Meade of the United States Naval Academy, and Jonathan Thompson were particularly meaningful to me. I am also grateful for Mike Gottleib's '70 talent and work in preparing the cover.

Others who offered support were Dr. Bob Lucking of Old Dominion University, CAPT Lewis's high school coach Terry McDonald, VADM Edward C. Waller '49, Navy's Turnbull Award recipients: Stewart McLean '48, Tom Mitchell '61, and Mike Buzzell '80, Bill Tanton, of *Lacrosse* magazine, Josh Christian of US Lacrosse, CAPT J.O. Coppedge '47, Dr. Shannon French of USNA's ethics department, Navy Hall-of-

Fame defenseman CDR Carl Tamulevich '68, Navy's "Stick Doctor" Tommy Adams, Bill Bilderback, Tim Nelson, Beverly McColley, Diane Glancy, Bonnie McEneaney, Jim Loeffler, Eric Ruden, my company- and classmate Mike Collins '84, CAPT Gerald Coffee, Al Bianchi, Sean Wetmore, J. Sills O'Keefe, Dr. John H. Tucker, Jr., Tom York, Toy Savage, LCOL Mike Horstman USMA '64, Dennis Manning, my parents, George and Teresa Duffy, my father-in-law Joe Finn, and Trent Blythe.

Two of my students and players, Mike Via and Jay Rixey, both of whom I coached for *six* years, were specially chosen to provide input from the player/student perspective. Gaines Frazier, another former student and player, was also gracious with his assistance.

Tom Duquette, Kathy Hobbs, and Dr. John Noffsinger provided invaluable editing assistance, correcting hundreds (maybe thousands) of spelling, grammatical, and style deficiencies, making the final product infinitely more readable. Jonathan Gullery provided the layout of the book. Mr. John O. "Dubby" Wynne's support has been invaluable.

ADM Charles R. Larson '58 has been an inspiration to me for many years, as have been my sponsors at USNA, LCOL (USMC) Mike and Cathy Sheedy, and their three wonderful daughters—my "adopted" sisters—Lisa, Jennifer, and Erin.

My sailors, students, athletes, and advisees over the last twenty years have been a constant source of inspiration and have given me much more than I could ever hope to give to them.

And, of course, I owe an eternal debt of gratitude to my wife, partner, and best friend, Jennifer, who for many years has patiently indulged my passion for the game of lacrosse and no less a passion for my students. It should go without saying that our children, Catherine and Drew, are the central source of hope and happiness in our lives.

This project could have easily withered or died at many

points. I was heartened and buoyed by the overwhelming and timely acts of kindness by all of these wonderful people. The completion of this project is as much a tribute to the generosity of others as it is to any of my humble efforts.

This journey has already been its own reward. The fact that you have now taken it makes it all the more special.

Thank you.

# About the Author

Neil Duffy is a native of Massapequa Park, Long Island. He is a graduate of Alfred G. Berner High School, the United States Naval Academy, and Old Dominion University. He is a teacher, coach, and advisor at Norfolk Academy in Norfolk, Virginia. He resides in Virginia Beach with his wife, daughter, and son.

Please share your thoughts and criticisms with the author at www.thespiritinthestick.com.